AF568079

ALEPH *olio*

THE BOOK OF INDIAN QUEENS

One of the meanings of the word 'olio' is 'a miscellany'. The books in the Aleph Olio series contain a selection of the finest writing to be had on a variety of Indian themes—the great cities, aspects of the country's culture and civilization, and other uniquely Indian phenomena. Filled with insights and haunting evocations of a country of unrivalled complexity, beauty, tragedy, and mystery, each Aleph Olio book presents India in ways that it has seldom been seen before.

Also in Aleph Olio

The Essence of Delhi
In a Violent Land
Love and Lust
Notes from the Hinterland
The Book of Indian Kings
Ways of Dying

THE BOOK OF INDIAN QUEENS

Stories and Essays

ALEPH

ALEPH BOOK COMPANY
An independent publishing firm
promoted by ***Rupa Publications India***

First published in India in 2023
by Aleph Book Company
7/16 Ansari Road, Daryaganj
New Delhi 110 002

The acknowledgments on p. 106 constitute an extension of the copyright page.

ISBN: 978-93-95853-12-5

1 3 5 7 9 10 8 6 4 2

Printed in India.

A NOTE ON THE BOOK

In order to preserve the form and flavour of the pieces as they were originally published, the texts have not been standardized according to Aleph's house style. In a couple of the pieces, notes, references, and cross-references have been excised.

CONTENTS

INTRODUCTION

'There was a time', writes the great historian of early India, Romila Thapar, 'when matrilineal societies were the accepted social pattern in the Indian subcontinent'. However, the era when women ruled India was disrupted by the 'coming of the Aryans' from Central Asia, 'who brought with them a patriarchal culture'. While the patriarchy would be the dominant feature of Indian society for centuries thereafter, the history of India is studded with stories of awe-inspiring queens (the descriptor 'queens' in this book covers all women who were rulers or of royal birth—empresses, queens, regents, princesses, begums, and so on). This book brings together some of the finest accounts in fiction and non-fiction on Indian queens from the earliest times to the present day, from every corner of the subcontinent.

Mahasweta Devi writes about Rani Lakshmibai in her final battle, Ruskin Bond tells the story of an enigmatic modern rani who has withdrawn from social life, Chitra Banerjee Divakaruni narrates the poignant tale of the last great queen of Punjab, Rani Jindan Kaur, Abraham Eraly recounts the exploits of the queens of classical India, Archana Garodia Gupta relates the story of Queen Didda, a controversial figure in the history of Kashmir, Ira Mukhoty brings Razia Sultan to life, Rudrangshu Mukherjee describes Begum Hazrat Mahal's entry in the freedom struggle, Ruby Lal provides insights into the empress Nur Jahan, Manu S. Pillai chronicles the maharani regents of Travancore who ruled as sovereigns, Binodini narrates the story of her rebellious aunt Princess Sanatombi of Manipur, and Gayatri Devi tells her own astonishing story.

Eye-opening and illuminating, the pieces in *The Book of Indian Queens* bring to blazing and visceral life the extraordinary women who moulded Indian history for hundreds of years.

ONE

~

THE RANI OF JHANSI

MAHASWETA DEVI

Translated from the Bengali
by Sagaree and Mandira Sengupta

Rani Lakshmibai is one of India's most celebrated historical figures who fought valiantly in the uprising of 1857. Widowed at a young age, Lakshmibai ruled as regent and refused to cede the kingdom of Jhansi to the British. This excerpt from Mahasweta Devi's The Queen of Jhansi *describes the fierce battle in Gwalior where Rani Lakshmibai commanded her troops against the British and was killed on the battlefield in 1858.*

Both the Indian and the English sides were watching Gwalior intently because they knew if Tatia Topi and the Queen defeated Hugh Rose in Gwalior the course of the war would turn around completely. If Gwalior stayed in Indian hands for too long, that would also have serious consequences for the British.

However, behind the scenes, the Indian leaders vacillated pathetically between hope and despair. At midnight on 12 June they were in for a rude shock when they received the news that Hugh Rose had reached Amin. A lack of mutual understanding had created a deep chasm between them. By the time they realized that wars cannot be won by mere physical might and patriotic spirit, but that knowledge of military tactics was also absolutely indispensable—things were already out of control. On the morning of 1 June, Tatia Topi became nervous as he tried to assemble the wildly upset soldiers. They had gathered under his banner without fearing for their lives because they had wanted a change of regimes; they had taken Gwalior, and what was their leader Tatia Topi doing but trying to gain credit by feeding brahmans!

At noon on 13 June, Rao Saheb, Tatia Topi and the Nawab of Banda came to the Queen. If they had paid any heed to what she had been saying all along during the battles of Kalpi, Kunch, Golaoli and Bahadurpur, they would not be in the position they were in now. The whole scene would have been different if they had not acted against her all the way in Gwalior and idled away their time in rituals and merrymaking. But it was too late now.

Surrounded by her attendants, the proud Queen sat solemnly with Damodar on her lap. The leaders were scared to approach her. Then Tatia Topi greeted her and said, 'The English are getting closer. We need to unite now and we need your help.' The Queen sighed and said, 'When you should have been preparing for war, you were absorbed in victory celebrations. What can I say? I am just an ordinary woman. But I am alarmed at the thought of what awaits us.' The leaders bowed their heads in self-reproach. Tatia Topi took his turban off and placed it in front of the Queen.

There was very little time to prepare or hope for victory, but the Queen still radiated enthusiasm and resolve. Tatia Topi left complete responsibility for Kotah-ki-Sarai to the Queen. She also took charge of the entire cavalry division. Hearing that she had accepted leadership, the soldiers felt hopeful again.

The Queen gathered together Raghunath Singh, Gul Muhammad, Ganpatrao Maratha, Ramchandra Rao Deshmukh,

Mandar, Kashi Kunbin, Juhi Natakwali, Nanna Khan and others who had come with her from Jhansi. She repeatedly entreated them to take Damodar away to safety at the least sign of danger. She also said, 'Please use the rest of my money and jewels to protect Damodar. He is a child but as I have opposed the English, they might torture this innocent boy. So, it is up to you to always keep him safe.'

She said to Damodar, 'Ananda, you are my only joy during these troubled times. You will be able to stay with Balarao, Kashi, Raghunath, and the others for some time when I'm not there, won't you? You should remember that I won't worry if I know that you are safe.'

The overwhelmed Damodar nodded in wonder. Although he had been given the name of the late infant crown prince Damodar at the time of his adoption, the Queen always called him Ananda. It was probably painful for her to call him by her dead son's name. She would always say, 'Ananda is my joy.' She also told her attendants not to be anywhere near the battlefields; they should not hesitate to escape if necessary. But they wondered, who was there to protect the Queen?

As if in answer to that unspoken question she asked Mandar, 'Bring my *shamsher* here.' Blue was her favourite colour. She tied a blue Chanderi *muretha* around her head and put on a blue angarkha or long fitted red shirt and close-fitting churidars. Around her neck was a pearl choker. Carrying the bejeweled sword in her hand and looking like the brilliant Goddess Gauri, she jumped on the horse Rajratna to go and inspect military processions on the fields of Kampu. The mare Sarangi had died in the Battle of Golaoli at Kalpi and Rajratna was presented to her by Bada Godbole Sagrid—a beautiful white horse bearing all the auspicious marks.

It was decided that Tatia Topi would form a front in Kampu, in the spot behind which the Sarasvat College is located now. Another of Tatia Topi's divisions would be to the north. Rao

Saheb would be in the west and the Nawab of Banda would remain in charge of Gwalior city and the fort.

Especially notable is the fact that the Queen was in charge of almost 10,000 soldiers at the crucial location of Kotah-ki-Sarai. The white-and-red shirted soldiers of the Gwalior Contingent were among them. The grey-pantalooned redcoats of the 5th Irregular (Regiment) also fought under her. At Kampu, the Queen and the Nawab of Banda drilled the soldiers. They did not want the defeats at Kunch and Golaoli repeated. The leaders were determined on this point. Fifty-eight cannons, big and small, were installed at various spots in Kotah-ki-Sarai Fort, Kampu, Phulbag and Morar.

On the dawn of 16 June, Hugh Rose reached Bahadurpur, four or five miles away from Morar. Learning of his progress, Rao Saheb had arrived in Morar on the evening of 15 June with several riders and cannons. Some select riders from Sindhia's troops were already there. Under Hugh Rose served expert warriors like Brigadier Steuart, Brigadier Napier, Captain Abbott, Lieutenant Neave, Lieutenants Harcourt and Strutt, Captain Lightfoot and Captain Rich.

Sir Robert Hamilton made Hugh Rose quite well-acquainted with the areas that were so familiar to him. He warned Hugh Rose repeatedly about the mountains and the gorges the Indians might be hiding in. On 16 June, marching towards Morar from Bahadurpur, Hugh Rose could feel distinctly that the river gorges on his left were teeming with enemy soldiers. Frequent barrages of cannonfire from Morar opposed his advance. On the British side, Lieutenant Neave was killed. After two hours of fierce fighting Hugh Rose took Morar. The Indians, although beleaguered, retreated in an orderly fashion. On the evening of 16 June, Lashkar sparkled brightly as innumerable torches lit up the place like day. An endless stream of people moved around in the bright lights.

The area between Kotah-ki-Sarai and Lashkar was filled with

gorges and ravines. Kotah-ki-Sarai had got its name from an inn. There was an insignificant fort, a river and a ditch here. It was also notorious for venomous snakes.

On 16 June, the Queen and the other leaders conferred all night and then several cannons were installed 1,50,000 yards away from Kotah, where the Mata-ki Mandir temple is now. Two divisions of soldiers were posted on the flat plains. Under Tatia Topi's direction, a frontline was organised on Kampu plain. Infantry, gun bearing soldiers, and cavalry were stationed in the ravines between Kotah and Lashkar. Mandar stayed in Phulbag with a troop. The Queen along with Raghunath Singh, took charge of the division between Phulbag and Kotah, and Gul Muhammad stayed in Kotah. In another spot presently known as Katighati, the Nawab of Banda waited with another army division.

Between 13 June and 17 June, the Queen hardly rested six hours a day. She was tireless. But her horse Rajratna was too tired to go on fighting. So at dawn on 17 June, she selected a fresh young horse from Sindhia's stable. Then, carrying her *shamsher* in her hand, a dagger at her waist, she dressed in white churidar and a red kurta just like the soldiers of the Gwalior Contingent. Due to her high military status, she put on her old pearl choker. She had received that necklace of pearls 15 years ago as a blessing from the Newalkars of Jhansi. She put on nagra slippers and tied a white Chanderi *muretha* around her head. Before dawn, she took leave of Damodar and reminded Ramchandra Rao Deshmukh, Ganpatrao and Kashi once more of her previous request. To honour that promise, these loyal and trusted followers remained under cover in a safe place.

There was no chance of rain; it began to heat up with sunrise. While riding towards the battlefield through a gentle morning breeze, she felt cheered and when she thought of the imminent battle, she felt joy. Busy soldiers here and there said to each other in reverence, 'There goes Bai Saheba!'

Brigadier Smith reached Kotah-ki-Sarai at 7 a.m. with various troops such as Her Majesty's 8th Hussars, 14th Light Dragoons, 95th Regiment, 1st Bombay Lancers, 3rd Troop Bombay Horse Artillery, 10th Bombay Native Infantry, and competent officers such as Colonel Blake, lieutenant Colonel Raines, Owen, Major Vialls, Meade (who was later responsible for Tatia Topi's execution), Lock, Heath and others.

He had no idea of the area's landscape but Smith could sense the Indian soldiers hiding throughout the distance between the mountain range and Lashkar. He had military rations and other equipment with him. He instructed the 8th Hussars and Bombay Lancers to store these in Kotah and stand guard there. They were supposed to stay right there and not budge unless absolutely necessary. Then Smith proceeded with extreme caution, keeping his eye on the ravines and gorges. Before he could advance 500 yards, the Indian cannons started blaring. After two barrages of cannon fire, Smith had to retreat. Then going forward with the Horse Artillery, he returned the barrage. The chief gunner on the Indian side was killed in the crossfire. After fighting for some time, the Indians began to retreat. Smith ordered Lieutenant Colonel Raines of the 95th Regiment to chase the Indians. Raines did so with both the 95th Regiment and the 10th Regiment Native Infantry. Gul Muhammad was among the Indians and while retreating with the Gwalior Contingent, he fired volley after volley of bullets to block the advance of the enemy. The Sonerekha ditch, with high sides and about four feet of water even then, lay in the way of the advancing troops of Raines. Their pace was checked. The cavalry and infantry crossed the ditch carefully, one at a time.

Meanwhile, Gul Muhammad moved away all the cannons and started returning towards Kampu by way of Lashkar. A second front of cannons, infantry, riders, and artillery had already formed a short distance away. Gul Muhammad stayed there and his troops retreated further back with the cannons. When Raines saw the enemy in front of him and was deciding what to do next, he noticed another division of the Gwalior Contingent on some high ground to his right. And immediately, his own division was bombarded with cannon balls by the enemy troops from the front and the side simultaneously.

When things began to look critical, Raines began to retreat. The 10th Regiment Infantry guarded the rear of his division. Major Vialls then joined the retreating Raines and they went together towards Kampu. But the English had to proceed under constant fire from the six cannons of Tatia Topi's troops. A furious battle between the English and the Gwalior Contingent ensued. Both sides were equally desperate and they fought for two whole hours, yet neither Raines and Vialls would budge nor did the Indians show any sign of slacking off.

The Indian flank began to break up at the end of two hours. The entire army of Indians retreated rapidly to the parade grounds of Phulbag. Phulbag had no walls around it then. So the areas to its front and back were also known as Phulbag.

As Raines marched towards Phulbag, he encountered another division 200 yards ahead. Raghunath Singh was with them. And immediately after that appeared another huge division led by the Queen herself and Mandar, with innumerable cavalry of the Gwalior Contingent.

The joint troops of Raines and Vialls were intimidated when they saw this front and fearing the worst, Brigadier Smith came from behind to assist with the entire 8th Hussar, the rest of the Light Dragoons and the Bombay Lancers. The 8th Hussar had not been engaged in any previous encounters so that it could fight during an emergency of this sort. Reassured, Raines stayed for an hour and then advanced again. An intense battle began.

The Queen cheered her soldiers and fought desperately herself. Her pearl necklace glistened. Nobody recognized her, because of her uniform. The English marvelled at her sword fighting skills, and thought she must be merely a skilful young male warrior.

The Queen, Raghunath Singh and Mandar advanced along with the Gwalior Cavalry while fighting. It was 3 p.m. on a blazing summer day. The battlefield resounded everywhere with the clanging of swords, the neighing of horses, the roar of cannons, the cries of the wounded and constant shouts and orders in Hindi and English.

Gradually, Raines' troops were scattered in disorder. Knowing victory to be certain, the Queen fought on unstoppably and her troops were fired up with her enthusiasm. The ferocious heat of summer was hard on the English and they began to lag behind. The atmospheric temperature was 125°F that day. Repeated shouts of '*Har Har Mahadev*' rose from the Indian camp. At that point of final crisis, Brigadier Smith ordered the 8th Hussar to attack.

The Queen's army was exhausted from continuous fighting. Alarmed at the rapid advance of the 8th Hussars, she ordered Mandar and Raghunath Singh to move on to the Phulbag encampment. Captain Heneage, Captain Poore and Lieutenant Reiley advanced to the left with the majority of the 8th Hussars and dealt the Queen and her soldiers running helter-skelter below the fort, a terrible blow. Some people believe that because of the fierce battle, this area of Gwalior became known as Katighati or chopping den.

The fort gunners showered the attacking English with cannonade and even under such dire circumstances, the latter fought heroically. In the meantime, Captain Heneage had killed the Indian gunners and seized three of the cannons in Phulbag camp. Chaos and utter confusion was let loose in the entire camp. With several cavalry and a few infantry, the Queen tried to form another wall of resistance outside the camp in a final, desperate attempt to save the day. But, the majority of soldiers, dishevelled and panic-stricken, were already escaping across the Sonerekha and taking roads to either Morar or the Fort. Colonel Hicks had penetrated Phulbag and the situation turned even more serious.

The Queen, Mandar and Raghunath Singh got separated

from the original division with little more than a dozen soldiers left to them. They were on the flat plains with the high ground to the sides. The expert warriors of the 8th Hussars pounced on them with tremendous force from their high perches. The English still had not realized that the Queen and her companion Mandar were actually women in male garb.

At this time of extreme danger, the Queen tried her utmost to cross the Sonerekha. At that very moment Mandar's chest was pierced by a bullet. Sadly, she said 'I'm leaving you, Bai Saheba—I guess we won't be escaping together!' The Queen turned her horse around in a split second and killed Mandar's killer. At the same moment, the garment covering her neck shifted and her pearl choker became visible. Suddenly she felt a sword strike her forehead, slashing the right side of her head up to the right eye. She tried to stop the bleeding with torn folds from her turban. Despite the blood gushing out in a jet, she struck her horse's belly to make it go onward. Finally, when the horse crossed the Sonerekha, a sudden bullet pierced the left side of her chest. She immediately fell over on the horse.

Her few remaining followers, such as Gul Muhammad, Ganpatrao Maratha, and Nanne Khan came and joined Raghunath Singh. Raghunath turned back and shot, aiming at the waist of Lieutenant Reily who had been pursuing him, but Reily had already collapsed from sunstroke and died very shortly thereafter. Without delaying there any longer, Captain Heneage's party left for the other side of the Phulbag camp.

The Queen's attendants began to search for her intently. But where was she? A little further ahead, across the Sonerekha where the ground was even, the Queen's horse was found, looking hither and thither. It was disturbed by the smell of blood and was flaring its nostrils and stamping the ground. Even from a distance, they could see the Queen bent over its back. Gul Muhammad ran out to take the reins of the horse, and, crying like a child, brought the Queen back. The deserted homestead of Gangadas

Bawa was nearby and there was a huge grass stack next to it. There they gently lowered the Queen from her horse and laid her on the ground. Ramchandra Rao Deshmukh and Kashi Kunbin brought over Damodar Rao. They repeatedly sprinkled water on the Queen's brow, face and eyes with a scarf soaked in the muddy water of Sonerekha.

Night was approaching. From far away noises of the battle winding down and cries of the wounded could be heard. Cannon balls and gunshots still exploded here and there.

The Queen regained consciousness. She looked at the faces of her grief-stricken attendants and the befuddled Damodar. Ramchandra Rao Deshmukh, a religious and pious brahman, always had a tiny copper vessel filled with Ganga water tied to his golden sacred thread. The Queen used to tease him about his persistence with this habit even on a battlefield. When he poured the Ganga water on the Queen's lips now, perhaps she remembered her jokes.

Then softly but clearly the Queen expressed her final wish: 'Be as loyal to Ananda as you have been to me. Pay my troops their salary out of my remaining jewellery and money. Make sure the foreigners don't get hold of my body after my death.' These were her last words. Immediately after, she breathed her last. It was as if she had held onto life so long only to speak those words.

TWO

~

THE ROOM OF MANY COLOURS

RUSKIN BOND

Ruskin Bond tells the story of an enigmatic rani who has withdrawn from social life.

Last week I wrote a story, and all the time I was writing it, I thought it was a good story; but when it was finished and I had read it through, I found that there was something missing, that it didn't ring true. So I tore it up. I wrote a poem, about an old man sleeping in the sun, and this was true, but it was finished quickly, and once again I was left with the problem of what to write next. And I remembered my father, who taught me to write; and I thought, why not write about my father, and about the trees we planted, and about the people I knew while growing up and about what happened on the way to growing up.

And so, like Alice, I must begin at the beginning, and in the beginning there was this red insect, just like a velvet button, which I found on the front lawn of the bungalow. The grass was still wet with overnight rain.

I placed the insect on the palm of my hand, and took it into the house to show my father.

'Look, Dad,' I said, 'I haven't seen an insect like this before. Where has it come from?'

'Where did you find it?' he asked.

'On the grass.'

'It must have come down from the sky,' he said. 'It must have come down with the rain.'

Later, he told me how the insect really happened to be there but I preferred his first explanation. It was more fun to have it dropping from the sky.

I was seven at the time, and my father was thirty-seven, but, right from the beginning, he made me feel that I was old enough to talk to him about everything—insects, people, trees, steam engines, King George, comics, crocodiles, the Mahatma, the Viceroy, America, Mozambique, and Timbuctoo. We took long walks together, explored old ruins, chased butterflies, and waved to passing trains.

My mother had gone away when I was four, and I had very dim memories of her. Most other children had their mothers with them, and I found it a bit strange that mine couldn't stay. Whenever I asked my father why she'd gone, he'd say, 'You'll understand when you grow up.' And if I asked him *where* she'd gone, he'd look troubled and say, 'I really don't know.' This was the only question of mine to which he didn't have an answer.

But I was quite happy living alone with my father; I had never known any other kind of life.

We were sitting on an old wall, looking out to sea at a couple of Arab dhows and a tramp steamer, when my father said, 'Would you like to go to sea one day?'

'Where does the sea go?' I asked.

'It goes everywhere.'

'Does it go to the end of the world?'

'It goes right around the world. It's a round world.'

'It can't be.'

'It is. But it's so big, you can't see the roundness. When a fly sits on a watermelon, it can't see right around the melon, can it? The melon must seem quite flat to the fly. Well, in comparison to the world, we're much, much smaller than the tiniest of insects.'

'Have you been around the world?' I asked.

'No, only as far as England. That's where your grandfather was born.'

'And my grandmother?'

'She came to India from Norway when she was quite small. Norway is a cold land, with mountains and snow, and the sea cutting deep into the land. I was there as a boy. It's very beautiful, and the people are good and work hard.'

'I'd like to go there.'

'You will, one day. When you are older, I'll take you to Norway.'

'Is it better than England?'

'It's quite different.'

'Is it better than India?'

'It's quite different.'

'Is India like England?'

'No, it's different.'

'Well, what does "different" mean?'

'It means things are not the same. It means people are different. It means the weather is different. It means trees and birds and insects are different.'

'Are English crocodiles different from Indian crocodiles?'

'They don't have crocodiles in England.'

'Oh, then it must be different.'

'It would be a dull world if it was the same everywhere,' said my father.

He never lost patience with my endless questioning. If he wanted a rest, he would take out his pipe and spend a long time lighting it. If this took very long I'd find something else to do. But sometimes I'd wait patiently until the pipe was drawing, and then return to the attack.

'Will we always be in India?' I asked.

'No, we'll have to go away one day. You see, it's hard to explain, but it isn't really our country.'

'Ayah says it belongs to the king of England, and the jewels in his crown were taken from India, and that when the Indians get their jewels back the king will lose India! But first they have to get the crown from the king, but this is very difficult, she says, because the crown is always on his head. He even sleeps wearing his crown!'

Ayah was my nanny. She loved me deeply, and was always filling my head with strange and wonderful stories. My father did not comment on Ayah's views. All he said was, 'We'll have to go away some day.'

'How long have we been here?' I asked.

'Two hundred years.'

'No, I mean us.'

'Well, you were born in India, so that's seven years for you.'

'Then can't I stay here?'

'Do you want to?'

'I want to go across the sea. But can we take Ayah with us?'

'I don't know, son. Let's walk along the beach.'

We lived in an old palace beside a lake. The palace looked like a ruin from the outside, but the rooms were cool and comfortable. We lived in one wing, and my father organized a small school in another wing. His pupils were the children of the raja and the raja's relatives. My father had started life in India as a tea planter, but he had been trained as a teacher and the idea of starting a school in a small state facing the Arabian Sea had appealed to him. The pay wasn't much, but we had a palace to live in, the latest 1938 model Hillman to drive about in, and a number of servants. In those days, of course, everyone had servants (although the servants did not have any!). Ayah was our own; but the cook, the bearer, the gardener, and the bhisti were all provided by the state. Sometimes I sat in the schoolroom with the other children (who were all much bigger than me), sometimes I remained in the house with Ayah, sometimes I followed the gardener, Dukhi, about the spacious garden.

Dukhi means 'sad', and though I never could discover if the gardener had anything to feel sad about, the name certainly suited him. He had grown to resemble the drooping weeds that he was always digging up with a tiny spade. I seldom saw him standing up. He always sat on the ground with his knees well up to his chin, and attacked the weeds from this position. He could spend all day on his haunches, moving about the garden simply by shuffling his feet along the grass.

I tried to imitate his posture, sitting down on my heels and putting my knees into my armpits, but could never hold the position for more than five minutes.

Time had no meaning in a large garden, and Dukhi never hurried. Life, for him, was not a matter of one year succeeding another, but of five seasons—winter, spring, hot weather, monsoon, and autumn—arriving and departing. His seedbeds always had to be in readiness for the coming season, and he did not had look any further than the next monsoon. It was impossible to tell his age. He may have been thirty-six or eighty-six. He was either very young for his years or very old for them.

Dukhi loved bright colours, especially reds and yellows. He liked strongly scented flowers, like jasmine and honeysuckle. He couldn't understand my father's preference for the more delicately perfumed petunias and sweet peas. But I shared Dukhi's fondness for the common bright orange marigold, which is offered in temples and is used to make garlands and nosegays. When the garden was bare of all colour, the marigold would still be there, gay and flashy, challenging the sun.

Dukhi was very fond of making nosegays, and I liked to

watch him at work. A sunflower formed the centrepiece. It was surrounded by roses, marigolds, and oleander, fringed with green leaves, and bound together with silver thread. The perfume was overpowering. The nosegays were presented to me or my father on special occasions, that is, on a birthday or to guests of my father's who were considered important.

One day I found Dukhi making a nosegay, and said, 'No one is coming today, Dukhi. It isn't even a birthday.'

'It is a birthday, Chota Sahib,' he said. 'Little Sahib' was the title he had given me. It wasn't much of a title compared to Raja Sahib, Diwan Sahib or Burra Sahib, but it was nice to have a title at the age of seven.

'Oh,' I said, 'And is there a party, too?'

'No party.'

'What's the use of a birthday without a party? What's the use of a birthday without presents?'

'This person doesn't like presents—just flowers.'

'Who is it?' I asked, full of curiosity.

'If you want to find out, you can take these flowers to her. She lives right at the top of that far side of the palace. There are twenty-two steps to climb. Remember that, Chota Sahib, you take twenty-three steps and you will go over the edge and into the lake!'

I started climbing the stairs.

It was a spiral staircase of wrought iron, and it went round and round and up and up, and it made me quite dizzy and tired.

At the top I found myself on a small balcony, which looked out over the lake and another palace, at the crowded city and the distant harbour. I heard a voice, a rather high, musical voice, saying (in English), 'Are you a ghost?' I turned to see who had spoken but found the balcony empty. The voice had come from a dark room.

I turned to the stairway, ready to flee, but the voice said, 'Oh, don't go, there's nothing to be frightened of!'

And so I stood still, peering cautiously into the darkness of the room.

'First, tell me—are you a ghost?'

'I'm a boy,' I said.

'And I'm a girl. We can be friends. I can't come out there, so you had better come in. Come along, I'm not a ghost either—not yet, anyway!'

As there was nothing very frightening about the voice, I stepped into the room. It was dark inside, and, coming in from the glare, it took me some time to make out the tiny, elderly lady seated on a cushioned gilt chair. She wore a red sari, lots of coloured bangles on her wrists, and golden earrings. Her hair was streaked with white, but her skin was still quite smooth and unlined, and she had large and very beautiful eyes.

'You must be Master Bond!' she said. 'Do you know who I am?'

'You're a lady with a birthday,' I said, 'but that's all I know. Dukhi didn't tell me any more.'

'If you promise to keep it secret, I'll tell you who I am. You see, everyone thinks I'm mad. Do you think so too?'

'I don't know.'

'Well, you must tell me if you think so,' she said with a chuckle. Her laugh was the sort of sound made by the gecko, a little wall lizard, coming from deep down in the throat. 'I have a feeling you are a truthful boy. Do you find it very difficult to tell the truth?'

'Sometimes.'

'Sometimes. Of course, there are times when I tell lies—lots of little lies—because they're such fun! But would you call me a liar? I wouldn't, if I were you, but *would* you?'

'Are you a liar?'

'I'm asking you! If I were to tell you that I was a queen—that I *am* a queen—would you believe me?'

I thought deeply about this, and then said, 'I'll try to believe you.'

'Oh, but you *must* believe me. I'm a real queen, I'm a rani! Look, I've got diamonds to prove it!' And she held out her hands, and there was a ring on each finger, the stones glowing and glittering in the dim light. 'Diamonds, rubies, pearls, and emeralds! Only a queen can have these!' She was most anxious that I should believe her.

'You must be a queen,' I said.

'Right!' she snapped. 'In that case, would you mind calling me, "Your Highness"?'

'Your Highness,' I said.

She smiled. It was a slow, beautiful smile. Her whole face lit up. 'I could love you,' she said. 'But better still, I'll give you something to eat. Do you like chocolates?'

'Yes, Your Highness.'

'Well,' she said, taking a box from the table beside her, 'these have come all the way from England. 'Take two. Only two, mind, otherwise the box will finish before Thursday, and I don't want that to happen because I won't get any more till Saturday. That's when Captain MacWhirr's ship gets in, the S. S. *Lucy*, loaded with boxes and boxes of chocolates!'

'All for you?' I asked in considerable awe.

'Yes, of course. They have to last at least three months. I get them from England. I get only the best chocolates. I like them with pink, crunchy fillings, don't you?'

'Oh, yes!' I exclaimed, full of envy.

'Never mind,' she said. 'I may give you one, now and then—if you're very nice to me! Here you are, help yourself…' She pushed the chocolate box towards me.

I took a silver-wrapped chocolate, and then just as I was thinking of taking a second, she quickly took the box away.

'No more!' she said. 'They have to last till Saturday.'

'But I took only one,' I said with some indignation.

'Did you?' She gave me a sharp look, decided I was telling the truth, and said graciously, 'Well, in that case you can have another.'

Watching the rani carefully, in case she snatched the box away again, I selected a second chocolate, this one with a green wrapper. I don't remember what kind of day it was outside, but I remember the bright green of the chocolate wrapper.

I thought it would be rude to eat the chocolates in front of a queen, so I put them in my pocket and said, 'I'd better go now. Ayah will be looking for me.'

'And when will you be coming to see me again?'

'I don't know,' I said.

'Your Highness.'

'Your Highness.'

'There's something I want you to do for me,' she said, placing one finger on my shoulder, and giving me a conspiratorial look. 'Will you do it?'

'What is it, Your Highness?'

'What is it? Why do you ask? A real prince never asks where or why or whatever, he simply does what the princess asks of him. When I was a princess—before I became a queen, that is—I asked a prince to swim across the lake and fetch me a lily growing on the other bank.'

'And did he get it for you?'

'He drowned halfway across. Let that be a lesson to you. Never agree to do something without knowing what it is.'

'But I thought you said...'

'Never mind what I *said*. It's what I say that matters!'

'Oh, all right,' I said, fidgeting to be gone. 'What is it you want me to do?'

'Nothing.' Her tiny rosebud lips pouted and she stared sullenly at a picture on the wall. Now that my eyes had grown used to the dim light in the room, I noticed that the walls were hung with portraits of stout rajas and ranis turbaned and bedecked in fine clothes. There were also portraits of Queen Victoria and King George V of England. And, in the centre of all this distinguished company, a large picture of Mickey Mouse.

'I'll do it if it isn't too dangerous,' I said.

'Then listen.' She took my hand and drew me towards her—what a tiny hand she had!—and whispered, 'I want a red rose. From the palace garden. But be careful! Don't let Dukhi, the gardener, catch you. He'll know it's for me. He knows I love roses. And he hates me! I'll tell you why, one day. But if he catches you, he'll do something terrible.'

'To me?'

'No, to himself. That's much worse, isn't it? He'll tie himself into knots, or lie naked on a bed of thorns, or go on a long fast with nothing to eat but fruit, sweets, and chicken! So you will be careful, won't you?'

'Oh, but he doesn't hate you,' I cried in protest, remembering the flowers he'd sent for her, and looking around I found that I'd been sitting on them. 'Look, he sent these flowers for your birthday!'

'Well, if he sent them for my birthday, you can take them back,' she snapped. 'But if he sent them for me...' and she suddenly softened and looked coy, 'then I might keep them. Thank you, my dear, it was a very sweet thought.' And she learnt forward as though to kiss me.

'It's late, I must go!' I said in alarm, and turning on my heels, ran out of the room and down the spiral staircase.

Father hadn't started lunch, or rather tiffin, as we called it then. He usually waited for me if I was late. I don't suppose he enjoyed eating alone.

For tiffin we usually had rice, a mutton curry (koftas or meatballs, with plenty of gravy, was my favourite curry), fried dal, and a hot lime or mango pickle. For supper we had English food—a soup, roast pork and fried potatoes, a rich gravy made by my father, and a custard or caramel pudding. My father enjoyed cooking, but it was only in the morning that he found time for it. Breakfast was his own creation. He cooked eggs in a variety of interesting ways, and favoured some Italian recipes which he had collected during a trip to Europe, long before I was born.

In deference to the feelings of our Hindu friends, we did not eat beef; but, apart from mutton and chicken, there was a plentiful supply of other meats—partridge, venison, lobster, and even porcupine!

'And where have you been?' asked my father, helping himself to the rice as soon as he saw me come in.

'To the top of the old palace,' I said.

'Did you meet anyone there?'

'Yes, I met a tiny lady who told me she was a rani. She gave me chocolates.'

'As a rule, she doesn't like visitors.'

'Oh, she didn't mind me. But is she really a queen?'

'Well, she's the daughter of a maharaja. That makes her a princess. She never married. There's a story that she fell in love with a commoner, one of the palace servants, and wanted to marry him, but of course they wouldn't allow that. She became very melancholic, and started living all by herself in the old palace. They give her everything she needs, but she doesn't go out or have visitors. Everyone says she's mad.'

'How do they know?' I asked.

'Because she's different from other people, I suppose.'

'Is that being mad?'

'No. Not really, I suppose madness is not seeing things as others see them.'

'Is that very bad?'

'No,' said Father, who for once was finding it very difficult to explain something to me. 'But people who are like that—people whose minds are so different that they don't think, step by step, as we do, whose thoughts jump all over the place—such people are difficult to live with.'

'Step by step,' I repeated. 'Step by step.'

'You aren't eating,' said my father. 'Hurry up, and you can come with me to school today.'

I always looked forward to attending my father's classes. He did not take me to the schoolroom very often, because he wanted school to be a treat, to begin with, and then, later, the routine wouldn't be so unwelcome.

Sitting there with older children, understanding only half of what they were learning, I felt important and part grown-up. And of course I did learn to read and write, although I first learnt to read upside-down, by means of standing in front of the others' desks and peering across at their books. Later, when I went to school, I had some difficulty in learning to read the right way up; and even today I sometimes read upside-down, for the sake of variety. I don't mean that I read standing on my head; simply that I held the book upside-down.

I had at my command a number of rhymes and jingles, the most interesting of these being 'Solomon Grundy'.

Solomon Grundy,
Born on a Monday,
Christened on Tuesday,
Married on Wednesday,
Took ill on Thursday,
Worse on Friday,
Died on Saturday,
Buried on Sunday:
This is the end of
Solomon Grundy.

Was that all that life amounted to, in the end? And were we all Solomon Grundys? These were questions that bothered me at the time. Another puzzling rhyme was the one that went:

Hark, hark,
The dogs do hark,
The beggars are coming to town;
Some in rags,
Some in bags,
And some in velvet gowns.

This rhyme puzzled me for a long time. There were beggars aplenty in the bazaar, and sometimes they came to the house, and some of them, did wear rags and bags (and some nothing at all) and the dogs did bark at them, but the beggar in the velvet gown never came our way.

'Who's this beggar in a velvet gown?' I asked my father.

'Not a beggar at all,' he said.

'Then why call him one?'

And I went to Ayah and asked her the same question, 'Who is the beggar in the velvet gown?'

'Jesus Christ,' said Ayah.

Ayah was a fervent Christian and made me say my prayers at night, even when I was very sleepy. She had, I think, Arab and Negro blood in addition to the blood of the Koli fishing community to which her mother had belonged. Her father, a sailor on an Arab dhow, had been a convert to Christianity. Ayah was a large, buxom woman, with heavy hands and feet and a slow, swaying gait that had all the grace and majesty of a royal elephant. Elephants for all their size are nimble creatures; and Ayah, too, was nimble, sensitive, and gentle with her big hands. Her face was always sweet and childlike.

Although a Christian, she clung to many of the beliefs of her parents, and loved to tell me stories about mischievous and evil spirits, humans who changed into animals, and snakes who had been princes in their former lives.

There was the story of the snake who married a princess. At first the princess did not wish to marry the snake, whom she had met in a forest, but the snake insisted, saying, 'I'll kill you if you won't marry me,' and of course that settled the question. The snake led his bride away and took her to a great treasure. 'I was a prince in my former life,' he explained. 'This treasure is yours.' And then the snake very gallantly disappeared.

'Snakes,' declared Ayah, 'are very lucky omens if seen early in the morning.'

'But what if the snake bites the lucky person?' I asked.

'He will be lucky all the same,' said Ayah with a logic that was all her own.

Snakes! There were a number of them living in the big garden, and my father had advised me to avoid the long grass. But I had seen snakes crossing the road (a lucky omen, according to Ayah) and they were never aggressive.

'A snake won't attack you,' said Father, 'provided you leave it alone. Of course, if you step on one it will probably bite.'

'Are all snakes poisonous?'

'Yes, but only a few are poisonous enough to kill a man. Others use their poison on rats and frogs. A good thing, too, otherwise during the rains the house would be taken over by the frogs.'

One afternoon, while Father was at school, Ayah found a snake in the bathtub. It wasn't early morning and so the snake couldn't have been a lucky one. Ayah was frightened and ran into the garden calling for help. Dukhi came running. Ayah ordered me to stay outside while they went after the snake.

And it was while I was alone in the garden—an unusual circumstance, since Dukhi was nearly always there—that I remembered the rani's request. On an impulse, I went to the nearest rose bush and plucked the largest rose, pricking my thumb in the process.

And then, without waiting to see what had happened to the snake (it finally escaped), I started up the steps to the top of the old palace.

When I got to the top, I knocked on the door of the rani's room. Getting no reply, I walked along the balcony until I reached another doorway. There were wooden panels around the door, with elephants, camels, and turbaned warriors carved into it. As the door was open, I walked boldly into the room then stood still in astonishment. The room was filled with a strange light. There were windows going right around the room, and each small windowpane was made of a different coloured glass. The sun that came through one window flung red and green and purple colours on the figure of the little rani who stood there with her face pressed to the glass.

She spoke to me without turning from the window. 'This is my favourite room. I have all the colours here. I can see a different world through each pane of glass. Come, join me!' And she beckoned to me, her small hand fluttering like a delicate butterfly.

I went up to the rani. She was only a little taller than me, and we were able to share the same windowpane.

'See, it's a red world!' she said.

The garden below, the palace and the lake, were all tinted red. I watched the rani's world for a little while and then touched her on the arm, and said, 'I have brought you a rose!'

She started away from me, and her eyes looked frightened. She would not look at the rose.

'Oh, why did you bring it?' she cried, wringing her hands. 'He'll be arrested now!'

'Who'll be arrested?'

'The prince, of course!'

'But *I* took it,' I said. 'No one saw me. Ayah and Dukhi were inside the house, catching a snake.'

'Did they catch it?' she asked, forgetting about the rose.

'I don't know. I didn't wait to see!'

'They should follow the snake, instead of catching it. It may lead them to a treasure. All snakes have treasures to guard.'

This seemed to confirm what Ayah had been telling me, and I resolved that I would follow the next snake that I met.

'Don't you like the rose, then?' I asked.

'Did you steal it?'

'Yes.'

'Good. Flowers should always be stolen. They're more fragrant then.'

∽

Because of a man called Hitler war had been declared in Europe and Britain was fighting Germany.

In my comic papers, the Germans were usually shown as blundering idiots; so I didn't see how Britain could possibly lose the war, nor why it should concern India, nor why it should be necessary for my father to join up. But I remember him showing me a newspaper headline which said:

> BOMBS FALL ON BUCKINGHAM PALACE—KING AND QUEEN SAFE

I expect that had something to do with it.

He went to Delhi for an interview with the RAF and I was left in Ayah's charge.

It was a week I remember well, because it was the first time I had been left on my own. That first night I was afraid—afraid of the dark, afraid of the emptiness of the house, afraid of the howling of the jackals outside. The loud ticking of the clock was the only reassuring sound: clocks really made themselves heard in those days! I tried concentrating on the ticking, shutting out other sounds and the menace of the dark, but it wouldn't work. I thought I heard a faint hissing near the bed, and sat up, bathed in perspiration, certain that a snake was in the room. I shouted for Ayah and she came running, switching on all the lights.

'A snake!' I cried. 'There's a snake in the room!'

'Where, baba?'

'I don't know where, but I *heard* it.'

Ayah looked under the bed, and behind the chairs and tables, but there was no snake to be found. She persuaded me that I must have heard the breeze whispering in the mosquito curtains.

But I didn't want to be left alone.

'I'm coming to you,' I said, and followed her into her small room near the kitchen.

Ayah slept on a low string cot. The mattress was thin, the blanket worn and patched up; but Ayah's warm and solid body made up for the discomfort of the bed. I snuggled up to her and was soon asleep.

I had almost forgotten the rani in the old palace and was about to pay her a visit when, to my surprise, I found her in the garden. I had risen early that morning, and had gone running barefoot over the dew-drenched grass. No one was about, but I startled a flock of parrots and the birds rose screeching from a banyan tree and wheeled away to some other corner of the palace grounds. I was just in time to see a mongoose scurrying across the grass with an egg in its mouth. The mongoose must have been raiding the poultry farm at the palace.

I was trying to locate the mongoose's hideout, and was on all fours in a jungle of tall cosmos plants when I heard the rustle of clothes, and turned to find the rani staring at me. She didn't ask me what I was doing there, but simply said: 'I don't think he could have gone in there.'

'But I saw him go this way,' I said.

'Nonsense! He doesn't live in this part of the garden. He lives in the roots of the banyan tree.'

'But that's where the snake lives,' I said

'You mean the snake who was a prince. Well, that's who I'm looking for!'

'A snake who was a prince!' I gaped at the rani.

She made a gesture of impatience with her butterfly hands, and said, 'Tut, you're only a child, you can't *understand*. The prince lives in the roots of the banyan tree, but he comes out early every morning. Have you seen him?'

'No. But I saw a mongoose.'

The rani became frightened. 'Oh dear, is there a mongoose in the garden? He might kill the prince!'

'How can a mongoose kill a prince?' I asked.

'You don't understand, Master Bond. Princes, when they die, are born again as snakes.'

'*All* princes?'

'No, only those who die before they can marry.'

'Did your prince die before he could marry you?'

'Yes. And he returned to this garden in the form of a beautiful snake.'

'Well,' I said, 'I hope it wasn't the snake the water carrier killed last week.'

'He killed a snake!' The rani looked horrified. She was quivering all over. 'It might have been the prince!'

'It was a brown snake,' I said.

'Oh, then it wasn't him.' She looked very relieved. 'Brown snakes are only ministers and people like that. It has to be a green snake to be a prince.'

'I haven't seen any green snakes here.'

'There's one living in the roots of the banyan tree. You won't kill it, will you?'

'Not if it's really a prince.'

'And you won't let others kill it?'

'I'll tell Ayah.'

'Good. You're on my side. But be careful of the gardener. Keep him away from the banyan tree. He's always killing snakes. I don't trust him at all.'

She came nearer and, leaning forward a little, looked into my eyes.

'Blue eyes—I trust them. But don't trust green eyes. And yellow eyes are evil.'

'I've never seen yellow eyes.'

'That's because you're pure,' she said, and turned away and hurried across the lawn as though she had just remembered a very urgent appointment.

The sun was up, slanting through the branches of the banyan tree, and Ayah's voice could be heard calling me for breakfast.

'Dukhi,' I said, when I found him in the garden later that day, 'Dukhi, don't kill the snake in the banyan tree.'

'A snake in the banyan tree!' he exclaimed, seizing his hose.

'No, no!' I said. 'I haven't seen it. But the rani says there's one. She says it was a prince in its former life, and that we shouldn't kill it.'

'Oh,' said Dukhi, smiling to himself. 'The rani says so. All right, you tell her we won't kill it.'

'Is it true that she was in love with a prince but that he died before she could marry him?'

'Something like that,' said Dukhi. 'It was a long time ago—before I came here.'

'My father says it wasn't a prince, but a commoner. Are you a commoner, Dukhi?'

'A commoner? What's that, Chota Sahib?'

'I'm not sure. Someone very poor, I suppose.'

'Then I must be a commoner,' said Dukhi.

'Were you in love with the rani?' I asked.

Dukhi was so startled that he dropped his hose and lost his balance; the first time I'd seen him lose his poise while squatting on his haunches.

'Don't say such things, Chota Sahib!'

'Why not?'

'You'll get me into trouble.'

'Then it must be true.'

Dukhi threw up his hands in mock despair and started collecting his implements.

'It's true, it's true!' I cried, dancing around him, and then I ran indoors to Ayah and said, 'Ayah, Dukhi was in love with the rani!'

Ayah gave a shriek of laughter, then looked very serious and put her finger against my lips.

'Don't say such things,' she said. 'Dukhi is of a very low caste. People won't like it if they hear what you say. And besides, the rani told you her prince died and turned into a snake. Well, Dukhi hasn't become a snake as yet, has he?'

True, Dukhi didn't look as though he could be anything but a gardener; but I wasn't satisfied with his denials or with Ayah's attempts to still my tongue. Hadn't Dukhi sent the rani a nosegay?

When my father came home, he looked quite pleased with himself.

'What have you brought for me?' was the first question I asked.

He had brought me some new books, a dartboard, and a train set; and in my excitement over examining these gifts, I forgot to ask about the result of his trip.

It was during tiffin that he told me what had happened and what was going to happen.

'We'll be going away soon' he said. 'I've joined the Royal Air Force. I'll have to work in Delhi.'

'Oh! Will you be in the war, Dad? Will you fly a plane?'

'No, I'm too old to be flying planes. I'll be forty years old in July. The RAF will be giving me what they call intelligence work, decoding secret messages and things like that and I don't suppose I'll be able to tell you much about it.'

This didn't sound as exciting as flying planes, but it sounded important and rather mysterious.

'Well, I hope it's interesting,' I said. 'Is Delhi a good place to live in?'

'I'm not sure. It will be very hot by the middle of April. And you won't be able to stay with me, Ruskin—not at first, anyway, not until I can get married quarters and then, only if your mother returns… Meanwhile, you'll stay with your grandmother in Dehra.' He must have seen the disappointment on my face, because he quickly added, 'Of course, I'll come to see you often. Dehra isn't far from Delhi—only a night's train journey.'

But I was dismayed. It wasn't that I didn't want to stay with my grandmother, but I had grown so used to sharing my father's life and even watching him at work, that the thought of being separated from him was unbearable.

'Not as bad as going to boarding school,' he said. 'And that's the only alternative.'

'Not boarding school,' I said quickly, 'I'll run away from boarding school.'

'Well, you won't want to run away from your grandmother. She's very fond of you. And if you come with me to Delhi, you'll be alone all day in a stuffy little hut while I'm away at work. Sometimes I may have to go on tour—then what happens?'

'I don't mind being on my own.' And this was true. I had already grown accustomed to having my own room and my own trunk and my own bookshelf and I felt as though I was about to lose these things.

'Will Ayah come too?' I asked.

My father looked thoughtful. 'Would you like that?'

'Ayah must come,' I said firmly. 'Otherwise I'll run away.'

'I'll have to ask her,' said my father.

Ayah, it turned out, was quite ready to come with us. In fact, she was indignant that Father should have considered leaving her behind. She had brought me up since my mother went away, and she wasn't going to hand over charge to any upstart aunt or governess. She was pleased and excited at the prospect of the move, and this helped to raise my spirits.

'What is Dehra like?' I asked my father.

'It's a green place,' he said. 'It lies in a valley in the foothills of the Himalaya, and it's surrounded by forests. There are lots of trees in Dehra.'

'Does grandmother's house have trees?'

'Yes. There's a big jackfruit tree in the garden. Your grandmother planted it when I was a boy. And there's an old banyan tree, which is good to climb. And there are fruit trees, litchis, mangoes, papayas.'

'Are there any books?'

'Grandmother's books won't interest you. But I'll be bringing you books from Delhi whenever I come to see you.'

I was beginning to look forward to the move. Changing houses had always been fun. Changing towns ought to be fun, too.

A few days before we left, I went to say goodbye to the rani.

'I'm going away,' I said.

'How lovely!' said the rani. 'I wish I could go away!'

'Why don't you?'

'They won't let me. They're afraid to let me out of the palace.'

'What are they afraid of, Your Highness?'

'That I might run away. Run away, far, far away, to the land where the leopards are learning to pray.'

Gosh, I thought, she's really quite crazy… But then she was silent, and started smoking a small hookah.

She drew on the hookah, looked at me, and asked, 'Where is your mother?'

'I haven't one.'

'Everyone has a mother. Did yours die?'

'No. She went away.'

She drew on her hookah again and then said, very sweetly, 'Don't go away…'

'I must,' I said. 'It's because of the war.'

'What war? Is there a war on? You see, no one tells me anything.'

'It's between us and Hitler,' I said.

'And who is Hitler?'

'He's a German.'

'I knew a German once, Dr Schreinherr, he had beautiful hands.'

'Was he an artist?'

'He was a dentist.'

The rani got up from her couch and accompanied me out on to the balcony. When we looked down at the garden, we could see Dukhi weeding a flower bed. Both of us gazed down at him in silence, and I wondered what the rani would say if I asked her if she had ever been in love with the palace gardener. Ayah had told me it would be an insulting question, so I held my peace. But as I walked slowly down the spiral staircase, the rani's voice came after me.

'Thank him,' she said. 'Thank him for the beautiful rose.'

THREE

~

RANI JINDAN KAUR

CHITRA BANERJEE DIVAKARUNI

Rani Jindan Kaur was the youngest wife of Maharaja Ranjit Singh. She ruled the Sikh empire as regent from 1843–1845 when her five-year-old son was named heir following the death of Maharaja Ranjit Singh and his successors. In this excerpt from The Last Queen, *set in 1839, Jindan Kaur is at the Maharaja's bedside, unaware of what her future holds.*

Jindan hasn't slept for two nights now, waiting by the sickbed of Maharaja Ranjit Singh along with his other wives. They've recited the Guru Granth Sahib until their throats are raw. *Birth and death are subject to the command of the Lord's Will… He who believes in the Name becomes victorious.* They've given away their finest Kashmiri shawls, jewels, cows, horses, elephants, sacks of gold coins. Jindan doesn't own as much as the other queens. She came to her marriage empty-handed and has never cared to cajole gifts from her husband. But she, too, has gifted a triple-stranded gold necklace to the Jagannath temple hoping for the recovery of the Sarkar, as his people lovingly call him.

She kneels on the marble floor, grateful for the stone's coolness, and rests her head against the carved gold bedpost. As the maharaja's youngest wife, and his favourite, she's allowed certain liberties. The other women sit straight-spined, palms joined stiffly. Some of them send her cutting glances from under their veils. She doesn't care. It's stuffy in this room with too much whispering, too many people—Hindustani vaids, European physicians, the senior courtiers, servants, priests, punkha pullers—and of course the wives, covered from head to foot as custom dictates. Above her head, the canopy bears down, a solid sheet of beaten gold. It oppresses her. Surely it oppresses the maharaja, too. He'd prefer to lie on the roof, she knows, in sight of the stars, as was his pleasure on summer nights. He'd breathe better there in the open with the city which he conquered and made his own stretching out beneath him. The intricate, beloved tapestry of Lahore, city of myth, fashioned from the wilderness before time began by Lav, son of Ram.

But to whom can she say this? Who will listen to her? The power she possessed even a few days ago, as the Sarkar's favourite queen, has faded.

In a corner of the chamber, the chief minister, Wazir Dhian Singh, his thin, sharp face chiselled from granite, stands still and stern though he must be as exhausted as they. More so, because he has been going back and forth every hour, informing the nobles waiting in the Diwan-i-Khas of the latest developments, reminding Kanwar Kharak Singh to stay close by so he can get to the chamber right away if the king calls for his eldest son and heir. Making sure the army is kept in readiness, just in case the British decide this is a good moment to cross the Sutlej River. In the city they whisper that were it not for Dhian Singh, the day the Sarkar dies the kingdom would shatter like a mud pot dropped by a careless housewife.

Dhian watches the doctors with keen suspicion as they administer medicines and poultices. Where his master is concerned, he trusts no one. When Ranjit Singh mumbles, he's the one who interprets the sounds rightly and strides forward with a lota of water. He holds the gold pot to the maharaja's lips, raising his head as tenderly as a mother. The maharaja takes a slow sip and whispers something. Dhian's eyes widen and, for a moment, dart towards Jindan. He looks troubled, but he touches the maharaja's hand to his forehead, a gesture of fealty. What is he agreeing to?

Jindan's temples pound. The mirror-tiles on the walls glitter mockingly. Bits of Dhian's story float up in her mind: how he came from distant Jammu, young and hungry, knowing no one in the big city. A common trooper, he caught the Sarkar's attention and rose rapidly, even though he wasn't Sikh but a Hindu. Her husband was always open-minded that way—quick to spot talent and even quicker to reward it. Perhaps that is why he invoked lifelong loyalty in so many men.

Jindan wishes the Sarkar would open his eyes. *Look at me*, she wills him. *Just once*. Then she feels selfish. *You don't need to look at me. Just open your eyes, that'll be enough*. How small he appears in the bed, as though he's shrunk in these few days. The women have started a new chant: *They who practise truth and perform service shall obtain their reward*. She joins them, lips moving automatically to the familiar words, but inside her head a different litany plays: *What will happen if he dies? What will happen to my baby, my Dalip, who is not even a year old?*

She pushes away that traitorous thought. The king has weathered worse. Illnesses, accidents, injuries, hunts and battles gone wrong, his thigh clawed by a tiger, a spear tip breaking off in his chest. Didn't he survive them? The smallpox in his childhood that took his left eye. The disease in the brain, a few years back, that caused him to fall to the ground, unable to move the left side of his body for days. Didn't he triumph over them all, ruling the greatest kingdom left in Hindustan? The only man with enough power to hold back the British? That's how it's sure to be again. A few weeks and he'll be laughing that raucous bark of a laugh, asking for his favourite horse, Laila, to be brought to him, feeding her lumps of jaggery with his own hands before springing onto her back. He'll be calling for more wine, more dancing girls, fireworks, pleasure boats, wrestlers, qawwaali singers ferried all the way from Lucknow. And after they've all left, it will be just the two of them, intertwined in the cool underground chambers of the Summer Palace, her lips travelling over his body the way he likes…

FOUR

~

THE QUEENS OF CLASSICAL INDIA

ABRAHAM ERALY

Women ruled as sovereigns, led armies, and played a crucial role in politics in several kingdoms of classical India. In this excerpt, the historian Abraham Eraly writes about stri-rajyas and the queens who ruled India as early as second century BCE.

Indian lawbooks and religious texts generally deny women any role in politics, and often speak in horror of women holding power. 'Infamous is the land where woman hold sway and rule; and infamous are the men who yield themselves to women's dominion,' warns *Jatakas*. But here again, as in much else in classical India, practice diverged greatly from prescription, and there are several historical instances of women ruling over kingdoms, even of leading armies in battle, and of men serving under them without any embarrassment. For instance, Megasthenes in India, at the close of the fourth century BCE, noted that queens ruled in the Pandya kingdom in South India. And, according to Hsuan Tsang, there was a kingdom in North India which had been 'for ages' ruled by women.

Some of the Puranas also speak of stri-rajyas, women's kingdoms.

The earliest specific historical instance of a queen reigning over a kingdom is of Nayanika of the Satavahana dynasty, who, in the second century BCE, ruled as regent for several years during the minority of her son. Half a millennium later, Queen Prabhavathi-Gupta ruled the Vakataka kingdom for many years as the regent of her infant son. In Orissa, too, there were instances of women ruling as regents, and even of princesses being crowned as rulers. In Kashmir, the wicked and power-mad queen Didda, in the tenth century, ruled for twenty all-too-long years as regent, by putting to death her sons one after the other as they came of age. And in the thirteenth-century Kakatya kingdom, the princess Rudramba succeeded her sonless father Ganapati and ruled for some thirty years by assuming the masculine title Rudradeva Maharaja. Writes Marco Polo: 'During all that space of forty years she … administered her realm as well as ever her husband (actually her father) did, or better; and as she was a lover of justice, of equity, and of peace, she was more beloved by those of her kingdom than ever was a Lady or Lord of theirs before.' Also in the thirteenth century, the queen Ballamahadevi of the Alupa dynasty in southern Karnataka ruled for many years with the masculine title Maharajadhiraja. Similar instances of women rulers are known in some other kingdoms as well.

Even when queens did not directly exercise power, they generally played a crucial advisory role in government from behind the scenes, and frequently issued orders directly to royal officers, particularly in making grants of religious charity. 'In all consultations and emergencies they take advice of the women,' notes Al-Biruni. In the peninsula, among the Chalukyas and the Rashtrakutas, royal women were generally given administrative and military training, and some of them took charge of provincial administration, and even of military operations. Thus, the Rashtrakuta princess Chandrobalabbe, daughter of Amoghavarsha I, served as the governor of Raichur; Umadevi, queen of the Hoysala king Viraballala II, sometimes commanded the royal army in its campaigns against rebel vassals; similarly, Akkadevi, sister of the Chalukya king Jayasimha II, often led the army in battle and supervised sieges when she was serving as provincial governor. In Kashmir, several queens are known to have done this.

FIVE

~

THE CONTROVERSIAL QUEEN OF KASHMIR

ARCHANA GARODIA GUPTA

Didda ruled Kashmir for fifty years from 958–1003 CE*. She was married to the ruler Kshemagupta and became regent upon his death. Didda quashed rebellions and dealt with several challenges to her power, including accusations of withcraft. Archana Garodia Gupta describes her reign in great detail.*

Unlike many other periods in ancient India, the history of Kashmir has been passed down to us in great detail thanks to the 12th-century chronicler, Kalhana, who describes it exhaustively in his work, *Rajatarangini*, written in 1149 CE. It is generally considered to be the oldest written history in India. It is brutally frank in its tales of blood and betrayal, and of kings of all castes - a clear indicator that it was not commissioned by the rulers themselves, who would have otherwise insisted on being mentioned as having appropriately glorious ancestors. To quote the historian R.S. Srivastava, 'In his history there are no heroes or heroines... Indeed, whether we love them or not for their virtues, it is their vices which make them unforgettable.'

At a time when rule by women was not supported either in Hindu or Buddhist scripture (in the Udyogparva in the Mahabharata Vidura goes so far as to say, 'The country where a woman, a child or a gambler rules, sinks helplessly as a stone raft in a river'), Kalhana mentions two queens who ruled before Didda. One was the mythical Kashmiri queen Yashovati, who was crowned with the support of Lord Krishna. Kalhana's comment on her saintly rule is this: 'The eyes of men which viewed womenkind with scant courtesy, considering it as one of the objects of their pleasure, looked upon this mother of her subjects as if she were a goddess.' The other woman ruler, Sugandhadevi, is known to have been in power just 50 years before Didda. She ruled at the beginning of the 10th century, first as a regent and then directly, though as the latter only for two years. Coins minted during her reign mention her as 'Sri Sugandhadeva' rather than 'devi'. Kalhana writes that she was overthrown and executed by her own courtiers.

At the beginning of the first millennium, Kashmir was a major intellectual centre for Buddhism, especially under Kanishka, the emperor of the Kushan dynasty. In the fourth and fifth centuries CE, hundreds of Kashmiri missionaries, among them the venerated Kumarajiva, travelled up the Karakoram Silk Route to spread the message of Buddhism to China. However, by the sixth century, Kashmir had been devastated by the invasion of the Hun ruler Mihirakula, who persecuted Buddhists and encouraged Shaivism. Kashmir, which had been the nursery of Buddhist scholars for hundreds of years, was now strongly Hindu. In the seventh and eighth centuries, the Karkota dynasty came to power in Kashmir. Its most powerful ruler, Lalitaditya Muktapida, created a brief Greater Indian empire when his troops raided lands as far as Assam, Afghanistan, Tibet, the Vindhyas, Gujarat and Sindh. He even had diplomatic relations with the Chinese emperor and offered to host 2,00,000 Chinese troops in Kashmir to fight their common enemy, the Tibetans. Fortunately, no Chinese troops showed up in Kashmir until the 20th century!

The Karkota dynasty was followed by the Utpala dynasty in the ninth century, which, after a brief moment of glory under King Avantivarman, became embroiled in civil war. The kingdom of Kashmir, which was now restricted to the Jhelum valley, was going through turmoil. The *damaras* (feudal landlords) and the *tantrins* (hired soldiers) frequently changed allegiance and constantly rebelled. Kings lasted but a few years and the people were left to the mercy of the government officials. Kalhana wrote, 'Truly, government servants are a plague to the people and harass them like cholera or dysentery.'

Parvagupta, a former minister of Kashmir, crowned himself king in 949 CE, killing the boy king Sangramadeva and throwing his body, weighed down with a stone, into the Jhelum. He, however, died painfully of dropsy (oedema) in just a year, leaving the throne to his son Kshemagupta. Kshemagupta was pleasure-loving and dissolute. He was addicted to women, gambling, and especially to hunting jackals in the woods, in a Kashmiri version of the British fox hunt.

It was during Kshemagupta's reign that Didda made an appearance. Didda's lineage can be traced back to the ancient and powerful Hindu Shahi dynasty who ruled Kapisa (now in Afghanistan) and Gandhara (which is in modern-day Pakistan) after the decline of the Kushan Empire, from the third to the 11th century CE. Her mother, daughter of King Bhima Shahi, was married to Simharaja, the king of Lohara (currently Lohrin in Poonch), a small kingdom adjacent to Kashmir.

Didda (b. 924 CE), the daughter of Simharaja, was beautiful but lame. She is often referred to as *charan-hina* (footless) in the *Rajatarangini*. Though she could walk, a woman called Valga would carry her around—even in running competitions. Didda would, of course, always win, as nobody dared to defeat the queen! In gratitude, Didda later built a *math* (temple) for her aide called Valgamath. Didda was still unmarried at twenty-six, very much over the marriageable age by the norms of the era, when Kshemagupta, looking for political legitimacy for his rule, offered to marry her, as she possessed the singular qualification of being the granddaughter of the mighty Shahis.

The wedding took place in 950 CE and Didda came to Srinagar as a bride. Soon her husband came under her spell so visibly that he started being taunted by the populace as 'Diddakshema'. Such was his infatuation that Kshemagupta had coins minted with 'Di(dda) Kshemagupta Deva' inscribed on them. Didda's influence over the king, however, created many enemies for her, among them the well-entrenched prime minister Phalguna, whose daughter Chandralekha was also married to Kshemagupta. Didda gave birth to a son, who was named Abhimanyu. When her grandfather, the powerful Bhima Shahi, visited Kashmir to see his great grandson he ordered the building of the temple known as Bhimakeshava near Martanda.

In 958 CE, Kshemagupta contracted a violent fever during one of his beloved jackal hunts. He was taken to the Kshemamath in Varahamula (now Baramulla) and died there. Panicking at the thought of what was to be her fate, Didda immediately secreted away her son, fearing he might be killed. She was now on her own, surrounded by threats to her son's life as well as her own. The first challenge came when the courtiers gathered for the king's funeral and, as per the prevailing royal custom, exerted pressure on Didda to commit sati along with the other queens, including Chandralekha, Phalguna's daughter. Didda staged a great show of preparing for sati, and at the last moment desisted on entreaties by some ministers to live on as her son was a minor. Her son Abhimanyu was then duly crowned and she became the regent. The prime minister, Phalguna, fearing for his life under Didda's rule, fled to Poonch.

Now set to rule the kingdom on behalf of her son, Didda was suspicious of everybody. The first direct challenge she faced was from Kshemagupta's nephews, Mahiman and Patala. They gathered many allies, especially powerful Brahmins from Lalitadityapur, and surrounded her while she was visiting the Padmasvamin temple. She managed to get her son away to a *math* and then asked for negotiations to commence. During the talks, she managed to ward off some of the allies with bribes and placate others. Her faithful minister, Naravahana, then won a victory in battle over the rest. She ruthlessly ordered the killing of many of the rebels, including her husband's nephews, but forgave some she thought would be of use to her. One of them was the warrior Yashodhara, whom she designated commander-in-chief, and sent off to subdue Thakkana, a king of Shahi descent who ruled a neighbouring kingdom. Yashodhara won, but let Thakkana retain his kingdom. When he came back, expecting a hero's welcome, Didda made an attempt to arrest him, possibly because the sight of a victorious army marching to the capital made her insecure about her throne, as it would any ruler, especially when the commander is known to have previously rebelled against the king. Many regime changes have been thus effected by victorious generals the world over, especially in Ancient Rome, the prime example being that of Julius Caesar. The attempted arrest, however, was botched up and Yashodhara immediately revolted, joined now by many nobles. This was perhaps the toughest revolt Didda ever faced, but she managed to suppress it with the help of her ministers, Naravahana and Rakka. Again, the rebels and their relatives were brutally killed.

Kalhana says of the crushing of the rebellion: 'The Lame Queen whom no one had thought capable of stepping over a cow's footprint got over the ocean-like host of her enemies just as Hanuman got over the ocean.'

Naravahana now became the most important man in the kingdom. Didda, increasingly nervous of his power, became aloof and started favouring others. Heartbroken, Naravahana committed suicide. In a little while Rakka too died. Didda, left alone again, could see the *damaras* uniting against her, and recalled Phalguna, who was living in retirement in Poonch, who then effectively subdued the *damaras*.

Meanwhile Abhimanyu was growing up and it seems was quite disturbed by his mother's shenanigans. As Kalhana put it, 'He was learned, his eyes had the beauty of lotuses, he was honoured by the sons of savants, he had studied the Vedas. He was asparkle with scholarship and youth. To one of such a very pure temperament co-operation with vile conduct proved withering, like the heat of the sun to the Sirisha flower.'

In 972 CE Abhimanyu died of consumption. His minor son Nandigupta was crowned king after him and Didda continued to rule as regent. For a year, a grief-stricken Didda immersed herself in constructing buildings in memory of her son. She built the Abhimanyusvamin temple and a town she named Abhimanyupura, as well as the Diddasvamin temple, Diddapura town and Diddamath, in a part of Srinagar now called the Diddmar area. She is credited with laying the foundations of 64 buildings in her lifetime.

Her run of bad luck continued through this time. Nandigupta fell sick and died within a year of ascending the throne, followed by the death of her next grandson, Tribhuvangupta, who had been crowned king the very same year. Many accused the queen regent of witchcraft and held her responsible for bringing about their deaths, though it seems quite unlikely, as she had no advantage in doing so. Undeterred, Didda now crowned Bhimagupta, her third grandson, the ruler of Kashmir in 975 CE. Phalguna, whom she had made her chief minister, died during Bhimagupta's reign.

Now began a new chapter in Didda's life, brought in by a young man called Tunga. Tunga was a Khasa buffalo herdsman from Poonch, who had come to Kashmir with his brothers and was employed as a letter carrier in Didda's administration. Impressed by his capabilities, she started promoting him to senior administrative posts, until he finally became prime minister and the commander of her armies. He continued to capably hold these posts for nearly forty years, even after her death. He was widely considered to be her lover, although she was over fifty years old by the time she met him.

Meanwhile, Bhimagupta was close to attaining adulthood and started showing interest in administration and reform. However, he died under mysterious circumstances in 981 CE, many say after being imprisoned and tortured by Didda. After his death, Didda ascended the throne in her own name and issued coins in the name of 'Sri Didda', which are widely available even today.

Didda ruled for the next 22 years with absolute power, quashing periodic rebellions by using her standard combination of bribes, placation and ferocious reprisal, until she died in 1003 CE at the age of 79. There is a story in Roman history about King Tarquin, who when asked by his son for advice on how to rule, goes to the garden and scythes off the heads of the tallest poppies. Didda did just this, with the faithful Tunga by her side, until there was no opposition left. She put down a major revolt spearheaded by her nephew Vigraharaja. Tunga and his brothers also won a major victory over Prithvipal, the king of Rajapuri (Rajouri).

Kalhana says of Didda, 'Those treacherous ministers who for sixty years... had robbed sixteen kings, from King Gopala to Abhimanyu, of their dignity, lives and riches, were quickly exterminated by the energy of Queen Didda.'

There is a quaint story about how Didda chose an heir. She called for many boys from her maternal family and placed a heap of fruits in front of them, challenging them to pick up the maximum number. The boys started grabbing the fruits and fighting with each other. In the end her brother's son, Samgramaraja, had the maximum number of fruits without actually engaging in any physical fighting. He had managed to incite the other boys to fight with each other while he calmly gathered up fruits. Impressed by his political acumen, Didda declared him her heir. She made Samgramaraja and Tunga swear a holy oath that they would work with each other, which created great stability in the kingdom for the next two decades.

Thus, Didda's maternal dynasty, the Loharas, established power in Kashmir, although according to the prevalent patriarchal norms, her heir should have been a blood relation of her husband rather than of her. When Mahmud of Ghazni attacked Kashmir, first in 1015 CE and then again in 1023 CE, Samgramaraja was one of the few kings in India to resist him successfully, in part because of the strong army and administration created by Didda, and partly because of the onset of winter.

The rule of the Lohara dynasty in Kashmir finally came to an end in 1320 CE with the savage attack of the Mongol chief Dulacha on Kashmir. The kingdom was devastated and plundered over eight months. However, while leaving with their loot, the Mongol army was destroyed to a man at the modern-day Banihal Pass by a fierce blizzard. Just like for Russia, winter proved an able general for the Kashmiris.

A new dynasty was then founded by Rinchan, a Buddhist from Ladakh, who later converted to Islam and took the name Sultan Sadruddin, becoming the first Muslim ruler of Kashmir.

Didda is a controversial ruler, who is difficult to slot into easy categories. All sources on her life and reign agree about her tremendous survival skills, her ruthless application of the maxims of the *Arthashastra*, her ability to rule and to select able lieutenants, and her success in achieving stability for the fractious kingdom she had inherited. However, her visible lust for power and snidely attributed obsession with the opposite sex, both considered admirable in men, were seen as failings and as an evil streak in a woman of her time. The innumerable lovers ascribed to her could well be due to gender bias by historians - after all, how else could a woman succeed in securing the loyalty of her ministers? Unless, of course, by witchcraft, which she was also accused of.

SIX

~

RAZIYA BINT ILTUTMISH, SLAVE TO SULTAN

IRA MUKHOTY

Raziya bint Iltutmish (r. 1236–1240) was the first and only female sultan of India. A remarkable administrator, she tactfully balanced opposing factions at court and ruled unaided by any man. Ira Mukhoty relates the circumstances that led to her ascension and her rule.

In 1205 CE, when the army of the unified tribes of Mongolia, the Khamag Mongol Ulus or the All Mongol State, rode across grasslands of the central steppes, they kicked up a gigantic column of dust that swirled about them. Along with the rumbling of thousands of hooves and the guttural war cries of the approaching horde their hapless victims would have heard the howling of Tibetan mastiffs, brought from their icy homes, adding to the nightmare. The leader of the horde was the Great Mongol Genghis Khan, the 'Scourge of God'. Within a few decades, the Mongols would have established the largest contiguous empire in the history of the world comprising all the lands between the Caspian Sea and Zhongdu or modern-day Beijing.

That same year, a girl was born to Iltutmish, the first ruler of the Delhi Sultanate, who would grow up to be Raziya bint Iltutmish, the Great Sultan, the first and only Muslim woman monarch in India. Remarkable as it might seem, the rise of the Turkish slave dynasty in Delhi and the enthronement of one of the first women in Islam, was a consequence of the rise of the Golden Horde of Genghis Khan.

From the tenth to the twelfth centuries in India, the development of urban centres slowly shifted westwards from Pataliputra towards the city of Kanauj, in the ancient Indian heartland of Madhya Desha. Kanauj was the great Hindu city of the early medieval period, consecrated by a monumental stone temple and governed by Brahminical orthodoxy and the heirarchy of caste. At this time, Muslim raiders and adventurers conquered the area of Sindh in the northwest, thereby securing the passage of goods to and from the Middle East. This created a porous frontier between the Islamic world—Dar al-Islam—and the 'pagan territory' or Dar al-Harb. As the authority of the Abbasid Caliphate slowly dwindled in Arabia, semi-independent amirs or governors grew in power; a faction controlled the Sindh province, plundering the riches of India including slaves, cattle, camels, goats, arms and other valuables. Among these opportunist plunderers was Mahmud of Ghazni whose India campaigns, it was said, 'were like bandit raids—he fought several quick battles, slaughtered enemy soldiers and people in multitudes, destroyed temples and smashed idols and sped back to Ghazni'. A century later, Muhammad Ghori crossed the Hindu Kush and challenged the Hindu kings of the north including, famously, Prithviraj Chauhan. These raids—like the earlier campaigns of Mahmud of Ghazni—left a trail of death and destruction in their wake. As soon as the short north-Indian winter spiked into the heat of spring, the raiders returned to the temperate climate of their homelands. For the Indian heat, as the sixteenth century scholar and historian Muhammad Khwandamir rather glumly stated, 'consumed the body as easily as flame melts a candle.'

At the same time, the formation of the Mongol empire was beginning to have devastating consequences for the people of Central Asia. The nomadic tribesmen of Genghis Khan spread through China and Central Asia razing cities to the ground and assimilating various nomadic tribes. Upon reaching the magnificent city of Bukhara, it is said, Genghis Khan ascended the pulpit at the Friday mosque and announced: 'O people, know that you have committed great sins, and that the great ones among you have committed these sins. If you ask me what proof I have for these words, I say it is because I am the punishment of God.' Ravaged and plundered, the Middle East returned to a nomadic lifestyle, its great cities reduced to dust and rubble.

China suffered too. It had thought itself invincible, guarded by its Great Wall to which six dynasties had contributed—it was twelve metres high and more than 10,000 kilometres long by the thirteenth century. But the Chinese underestimated the Mongol forces, who burst through gaps in the Great Wall and captured Zhongdu (later Peking and now Beijing). Fortunately, the natural barrier to the northwest of India—the Himalayas—from where the Mongols could have entered the country, was not so easy to penetrate, which was one of the reasons India was spared a similar fate. There was another reason India escaped a large-scale invasion by the Mongols and that was the sturdy Central Asian horse. The great strength of the Mongol horde was also its greatest weakness. Indispensable to the success of the Mongolian tribesmen was their cavalry. Six out of every ten Mongol troopers were mounted archers. Trained from childhood in horsemanship and archery, the Mongols were redoubtable fighters. Clad in light armour, unlike their contemporaries the crusader knights, they were extremely manoeuvrable, quick and mobile. Each Mongol soldier typically maintained three or four horses, changing mounts as they tired. This enabled them to cover huge distances at disconcerting speed. The drawback of this system was that it required a steady and continuous supply of grasslands as pasture for the horses. In India there were no grasslands, only the Hindu Kush, the Thar Desert, and then dense forests and marshy lands further east. In addition to these topographical factors, the presence of the Delhi Sultanate in northern India during the entire period of Mongol supremacy ensured that the nomad armies were kept at bay.

Instead of a Mongol invasion, a corridor opened up between the eastern Islamic world and India. In addition to the regular intrusion by a Muslim elite through the frontier lands, the arrival of people fleeing the Mongol hordes in Central Asia now added to the influx of peoples into India. In the early decades of the thirteenth century, the occasional trickle became a swarm as Delhi became a land of safety and refuge for armies, princes, scholars and artisans from all over Turkestan, Khorasan and Afghanistan. This led to a great mingling of cultures—Persian, Iranian, Turkish and Hindustani—and the exchange of habits, languages, food, music and architecture that would lead, in time, to the magnificent Indo-Islamic composite culture. In the immediate future, however, this converging of people led to the formation of the Delhi Sultanate: a Turkish tribe of slaves who became kings and enthroned the first and only female Sultan of India.

Turks had been recruited as military slaves since the ninth century, when the Abbasid caliphs used them as an elite guard corps in their capital cities. As the power of the caliphs disintegrated, the rising independent amirs used them to shore up their own reigns. By the ninth century, Turkish slaves formed a part of most armies in the Middle East including on Islam's Indian frontier but it was Muhammad Ghori who was most enthusiastic in acquiring them. When he died, in 1206, the rule of his Indian territories fell to his senior slaves and one of them, Qutb-ud-Din, made himself ruler of Lahore from where he controlled much of Pakistan and north India. But Qutb-ud-Din died, falling from his horse, only four years later and in 1210 it was his own slave, Shams-al-Din Iltutmish, who seized the throne and made Delhi the capital of his empire, becoming the first ruler of the Delhi Sultanate—the leading, and sometimes the only, Muslim-ruled state in India for the next two hundred years.

Shams al-Din Iltutmish died of natural causes in 1236 after a reign of twenty-five years. By then, his first-born son and heir apparent, Malik Nasir al-Din, was also dead. Clamouring for the throne of Iltutmish were his oldest surviving son, Rukn al-Din, a dilettante with a concupiscent interest in adolescent boys who was being supported by his mother, a vicious woman by all accounts; his third son, Ghiyas al-Din, commander of Awadh; and unconventionally, for the time, his twenty-nine-year-old unmarried daughter, Raziya. However, the most powerful and volatile player in the mix at this time was not an individual, but a group of men called the Chalisa (the Forty)—the experienced senior slaves among Iltultmish's retinue, also known as the Shamsi Bandagan, military slaves, or Bandagan-i-Khas, the elite slaves.

The rise of the Shamsi Bandagan, essentially a political coalition of slave soldiers, was a phenomenon unique to the Delhi Sultanate. Through the early decades of the thirteenth century, as the ghulams or satraps were given military command of annexed urban centres, they established slave retinues of their own to help them in their campaigns. As the elite ghulams distinguished themselves through acts of valour or loyalty, or through a personal kinship with the sultan, they rapidly advanced through the Bandagan hierarchy. Unlike in all the other regions of the world in which slavery existed, in the Delhi Sultanate a past as a slave was never a barrier to promotion. The historian Sunil Kumar has pointed out that by the end of Iltutmish's reign in 1236, the influence of the Turkish Bandagan on the political structure of the Sultanate was quite disproportionate to their number and social status.

When Muhammad Ghori formed his Bandagan, they were led by a corps of military slaves of largely Turkish ethnic background, assigned to protect the life of the sultan during military campaigns.

Kumar writes that by 'reputation at least, during moments of military crisis, they stood by their master and were the last to retreat.' These slaves, usually procured at a very young age, would have been trained so that they could gradually be given military responsibilities. Removed from the land of their birth and their ethnic origins, they were made to undergo a process of 'natal alienation and social death' that would ideally lead to the creation of strong new ties to each other and to the service of their master, the sultan. Along with their military training, the slaves were given religious instruction in Islam, and tutored in etiquette so they could interact with the sultan and his family without causing too much distress to their royal masters. Some of these slaves were new recruits and trained by the sultans or previously trained by slavers in which case they were much more valuable. Iltutmish, for instance, was highly valued because of 'his comeliness, his fairness, and agreeable manners'. The slavers felt that 'the further (the Turk slaves) are taken from their hearth, their kin and their dwellings, the more valued, precious and expensive they become and they become commanders and generals.' A seventeenth-century Englishman visiting Turkey described this succinctly by saying that 'the Turk loves to be served by his own, such as to whom he hath given breeding and education...and whom he can raise without envy and destroy without danger.' But the danger did exist, as the sultans of Delhi were to find out. As the ties with Ghazni and Afghanistan became increasingly fragile in the thirteenth century, the ghulams of the Bandagan-i-Khas became independent, powerful and ambitious.

When Iltutmish died in 1236, he had already been ailing for a few months and would have taken measures to ensure a smooth transition of power to his successors. Later biographers like Minhaj-i-Siraj Juzjani have claimed that Iltutmish named Raziya his successor because he is reported to have said: 'My sons are devoted to the pleasures of youth, and not one of them is qualified to be king. They are unfit to rule the country, and after my death you will find that there is no one more competent to guide the State than my daughter.' However, no textual evidence exists to back this statement and it is more likely that he promoted his oldest surviving son, Rukn al-Din, whom he appeared to be grooming for leadership, after the death of his first-born son, by giving him the governorship of Lahore. But within months of assuming power and having shifted his residence to the fortified town of Kulukhri, Rukn al-Din was facing revolt from various factions in his court including one from the senior ghulams of the Bandagan and some free amirs of the court. At the same time, his mother, Shah Terken, used her son's ascension to settle old scores in the harem and also had one of Rukn al-Din's half brothers blinded and put to death. It was when she tried to kill Rukn al-Din's half-sister, Raziya, whom she saw as a threat to her son's claim to the throne, that we first hear of the princess who would become the most powerful woman of al-Hind.

Ibn Battuta, writing a century after the event, describes the events that followed Rukn al-Din's attempt to assassinate Raziya: 'She presented herself to the army and addressed them from the roof saying, "My brother killed his brother and he now wants to kill me." Saying this, she reminded them of her father's time and of his good deeds and benevolence to the people.' With this claim to the memory of her father, Sultan Iltutmish, Raziya then asked for justice against Rukn al-Din and his mother. The crowds rallied around her, they stormed the palace and 'he [Rukn al-Din] was killed in retaliation for his brother's death.' Following this, 'the army agreed to appoint Raziya as ruler.'

When Raziya ascended the throne of Delhi in this tumultuous manner, she stood alone without a man beside her—no father, husband or son—asking men to revolt on her behalf at a time when affluent Muslim women were not meant to be seen in public. In the ninth century itself, the Iraqi theologian Al-Jahiz had categorically stated that 'the only purpose of high walls, stout doors, thick curtains, eunuchs, handmaidens and servants is to protect them [women] and to safeguard the pleasure they give.'

~

There is very little we know about the physical appearance of Raziya, apart from her gender. Standing on the steps of the kusk-i-firuzi or royal residence, she would have been wearing a tunic with long sleeves and a loose fitting shalwar covering her legs and feet. As it was the month of spring, she may have been wearing bright silks embroidered with gold threads. At this stage of her career we know that she was 'veiled from the public gaze', so she would have had a light gauze cloth drawn across the lower half of her face. Her physical features are lost to us since biographers, perfunctory at best even in describing their male subjects, were either silent or censored such details where women were concerned. We do know, however, that she was ethnically Turkish so it is likely that Raziya had the high cheekbones, wind-blown complexion and almond eyes characteristic of the people of the steppes.

Having roused the people of Delhi and foiled the attempt on her life, Raziya now had to confront the competing interests of the free Turkish noblemen, amirs from tribes such as the Khalaj, Ghuris, Tajiks and also some Mongols. Allegiances were made and then paid for in blood when they failed to pay off. The violence that defined succession politics in the Delhi Sultanate had much to do with the particular nature of the Turkish slaves. Recruited as military mercenaries, although they were malleable and ferocious warriors they could often prove to be dangerous to those who used them.

While unquestioned loyalty to the master was one of the primary attractions of a slave retinue, there were times when the reality was different. Raziya's father Iltutmish, himself a slave, carefully promoted after years of training, acted with savage and murderous disloyalty at the death of his king and benefactor, Qutb ud-Din. Qutb ud-Din had nominated his son Aram Shah to take over as Sultan upon his death, but it was his beloved slave Iltutmish—in whom 'the signs of rectitude were, time and again, manifest and clear in his actions and thoughts'—who seized the throne for himself. Iltutmish had spent years as military commander in the provinces of the Sultanate and had acquired a large and carefully trained following of soldiers himself. Backed by these soldiers, he made his move when the time was right, despite opposition from the free amirs as well as some of the other senior ghulams, who baulked at the idea of serving under one of their own. Later chroniclers were clearly uncomfortable about Iltutmish's actions and preferred to skate over this episode, almost eliding Aram Shah from history. That a much valued and loyal slave, supposed to protect the Sultan and his family with his own life, should so quickly and unequivocally destroy his master's lineage was an abomination. Sensing the magnitude of the opposition to his move, Iltutmish added legitimacy to his claim by marrying a princess—Qutb ud-Din's daughter.

When Iltutmish died, his ghulams—especially the Bandagan-i-Khas—had to decide whether to transfer their loyalty to the heirs of their master who had trained them and raised them to positions of power. Reputations and cliques formed over a quarter of a century of negotiations and advancements suddenly disappeared overnight. The prerogative of the elite of the Bandagan-i-Khas was to maintain their power structures as fiercely as possible. This brought them immediately and violently into opposition with the free amirs and the heirs to the throne who wanted to realign the balance of power.

After Rukn al-Din had been deposed, the ghulams of the court who had rebelled against him now installed Raziya on the throne. These slaves undoubtedly believed that a woman—and one who had until then lived in seclusion—would be malleable and would maintain the status quo they had enjoyed under Iltutmish's reign. Raziya's behaviour in the coming months would prove what a grave error of judgement this was.

The first measure Raziya took was to neutralize the threat from some of the senior amirs who had challenged Rukn al-Din's authority. These powerful nobles and ghulams had fallen out of favour with Iltutmish or Rukn al-Din and were therefore interested in creating chaos that they could use to their advantage. Soon after Raziya's ascension, they laid siege to Delhi. Among this group were the senior ghulam Kabir Khan, the freeborn amirs Ala al-Din Jani and Izz al-din Muhammad Salari, and Wazir Junaidi. Raziya showed enormous skill in handling these fractious warlords. She appeased Kabir Khan with the governorships first of Lahore and then Multan and won over Muhammad Salari; when the others proved recalcitrant, she did not hesitate in using stronger tactics—she had Ala al-Din Jani killed and the wazir forced into retirement.

Once the immediate threat of revolt had been taken care of Raziya turned her attention to the junior ghulams, the so-called 'Turks of the court'. These slaves, the original Shamsi slaves of Iltutmish, became crucial players in the politics of the Delhi Sultanate. Apart from their indispensable role in the armies, some of the more valued ghulams were given high office at the court of the sultans. They had ceremonial roles such as cupbearer, holder of the royal parasol or administrator of the royal stables. Raziya rewarded loyal ghulams and amirs with these positions. Junior slaves who had supported her during the revolt of the older ghulams, obtained high office and recognition for the first time. Thus Balaban 'the Lesser' was promoted from falconer to chief huntsman. Ikhtiya al-Din Altunia, a slightly more senior slave, was given the governorship of Barain, and Ikhtiyar al-Din Aytegin was given the coveted post of amir-hajib (sometimes translated as 'Lord Chamberlain'). Aytegin and Tughril Khan, who would have been on the verge of high office at the time of Iltutmish's death, now became, in effect, the Bandagan-i-Khas. Rather ominously though, as opposed to the old Bandagan-i-Khas under Iltutmish, they did not have their power granted to them by the Sultan but rather 'reached their powerful positions by holding the Sultan [Raziya] hostage.'

While rewarding crucial members of the Shamsi ghulams, Raziya was equally careful to patronize the non-Shamsi ghulams and Turks. Like Rukn al-Din before her, she was desperate to break the monopoly of the ghulams at court. When the Turkish commander of the guard, Sayf al-Din Aybeg, died his post was given to a Ghuri Malik, Qutb al-Din Hasn. She gave the strategic governorship of Barain to the son of Hasan Qarluq, the Khwarazmian nobleman whom she had welcomed to her court.

Eminent noblemen had been drifting into the court of the Delhi Sultanate since the time of Iltutmish, fleeing the Mongols and other raiders or seeking advancement and opportunities. The Khwarazmian empire had been decimated after a Mongol caravan sent on a friendly mission was slaughtered by the Khwarazmians. Enraged, Genghis Khan himself led his armies to war and directed the destruction of the fabled cities of Samarkhand and Bukhara. When Sultan Jalal al-Din Khwarazm Shah sought sanctuary at Iltutmish's court, the Sultan refused probably wisely deciding against drawing the attention of Genghis Khan. Iltutmish also preferred to promote the 'socially dead', who would remain dependent on his patronage and were unlikely to create alternative power bases. Raziya, on the other hand, could not count on the unquestioned loyalty of the Shamsi ghulams or the free amirs. She had to maintain a delicate balance between different factions at court and in the provinces. In transferring the ghulams and amirs, she was making sure, like her father before her, that the men did not form powerful local ties within their domains.

Juzjani tells us that once these rebellions were quelled, 'the kingdom became pacified and the power of the state widely extended...all the Maliks and Amirs manifested their obedience and submission.' Even Isami, the fourteenth century historian writing a hundred years later about Raziya's reign, said that '[the] renowned woman threw herself into the tasks of administration and men of experience firmly resolved to serve her.' 'She ruled as an absolute monarch for four years,' added Ibn Battuta. 'She mounted horse like men armed with bow and quiver; and she would not cover her face.'

Raziya could now redirect her energy to ruling her kingdom and holding court at the kusk-i-firuzi at Mehrauli. The court was a public assembly and Raziya would have sat on a throne, a large, high-backed chair with a red canopy above it, flanked by a bodyguard of slaves armed with swords. In her court, there would have been Tajik bureaucrats, Persian adventurers and noblemen, holy men, scholars and Indian Muslims and other assorted Turkish and non-Turkish tribesmen. From the chronicles of the Ghaznavid Bayhaqi we can guess at what the slave guards, Central Asian men with high cheekbones and long black hair coiled in braids, would have been wearing: 'rich robes, bejeweled belts and sashes, and weapons decorated with gold and silver.' They would have been carrying maces, their traditional weapon, as well as various other items suspended from their belts, including a wallet, in the Central Asian fashion.

Isami has noted that Raziya's throne was initially separated from the courtiers and the public by a screen and that there were female guards standing next to her, as she was nominally still in purdah at the beginning of her reign. Later on, she would have sat in full view of the court, listening to her supplicants' entreaties and dispensing quick justice. In the evenings she would have attended the durbar where she would have witnessed a great alchemy of musical genres—Indian, Persian, classical and folk. There would have been scholars, artisans and performing artistes from the major centres of Islamic culture. Slaves would have walked around offering betel leaves to those present and the evenings would have culminated in banquets of chicken, goat, rice, roast beef and breads.

∽

The kingdom Raziya inherited from her father stretched from Delhi in the west to Lakhnauti in Bengal to the east. Under Raziya's reign, the autonomy of some of the eastern territories was virtually conceded to the powerful muqta of Lakhnauti, Toghan Khan. In dealing with independent powers, she was pragmatic. The fortress of Ranthambore had been under siege by the Chauhans for some time when Raziya came to power. She sent a force under Qutb al-Din Hasan to evacuate the Muslim garrison posted there and to destroy all the fortifications the Muslims had built. Similarly, in Gwalior, Sanajr-i-Qabaqulaq secured the Muslim population and brought them back to Delhi. Both Ranthambore and Gwalior passed back into the hands of Hindu kings—a reality the older Shamshis, for whom these had been major conquests, would have bitterly resented.

Iltutmish had also had a new system of coinage launched, based on the pure silver tanga which would eventually replace the dihliwals minted by the Hindu rulers of Delhi. Raziya had these coins minted with her own titles. Initially, these coins carried both her father's name as well as hers, proclaiming Iltutmish as Sultan al-Azam (the Greatest Sultan) and herself with the subordinate title of Sultan al-Mu'azzam (the Great Sultan), and reinforcing her legitimacy as Bent-al-Sultan (Daughter of the Sultan). In the early years of her reign she would have needed the weight of her father's title, but by 1238 Raziya had grown enough in confidence to have the coins minted in her own name: Al-Sultan al-Muazzam Radiyyat al-Din. Cultural historian and writer Alyssa Gabbay notes that 'she appears both on the coins and in the early histories with the gender-neutral and awe-inspiring sobriquet of Sultan: the king, the leader.' In her own lifetime, Raziya never opted for the title 'Sultana', the queen, an adjunct to the male power, the king.

At some point during her reign, Raziya abandoned purdah. Juzjani tells us that 'the sultan put aside female dress, and issued from [her] seclusion, and donned the tunic, and assumed the head-dress [of a man], and appeared among the people.' Raziya's appearance, though, would not have altered drastically as the Muslim garb for both men and women at the time was fairly similar and modest—a long tunic and loose pants. However, Raziya appeared in public with the quba (ceremonial cloak) and the kulah (pointed Turkish hat). Without her veil 'when she rode out on an elephant, at the time of mounting it, all people used, openly, to see her.' The removal of the veil was essential for Raziya to dissociate herself from being simply a female, and as such, 'naqes al-aql, deficient in intelligence, and therefore more prone to evil than men.' Without the veil the people could see more clearly the face of kingship, of power and of military strength. In the sixteenth century, Rani Durgawati dressed as a soldier to fight Akbar's Mughal troops and six hundred years after Raziya, Rani Laxmibai of Jhansi would also abandon feminine garb when she rode into battle against the British colonizers. Both Rani Durgawati and Rani Laxmibai, however, were dowager queens fighting for the rights of their infant sons. Raziya's claim to being Sultan was her conviction that she was the most capable of her siblings.

Alyssa Gabbay has argued that Raziya was part of a long line of Muslim women, including the Sassanian queens of Boran and Azarmidokht, who discarded their female attire as monarchs. In the subcontinent, however, such examples are rare. Though gender identities are more porous than those in the West, it is usually the men who cross-dress. Arjuna in the Mahabharat dresses as a woman and mistress of dance when he lives disguised as a eunuch in King Matsya's court as part of the terms of his exile. There is a great tradition of mystics, such as Ramakrishna and Chaitanya Mahaprabhu, dressing as women to symbolize the ideal devotee. Indeed, in Sufi mysticism as in Buddhism and Hinduism, the only 'true male' or purusha is God, everyone else must approach Him with the humility of a woman. It is as though a man's virility is inviolable, sacrosanct and the wearing of women's clothes is just a game, which never fundamentally challenges that virility; but when a woman wears a man's clothes a fault line appears in society.

By promoting the Ghurids and Khwarazmians and giving the powerful office of intendant of the imperial stables (Amir-i-Akhuri), to an outsider, Raziya was trying to curb the influence of her father's ghulams following his example of distributing power between loyal personages unlikely to have powerful local ties. The man she chose was an Abyssinian, an African malik called Jamal al-Din Yaqut. Therefore, when Raziya chose to elevate Malik Yaqut, she was following her father's example in distributing power between strong and loyal personages unlikely to have powerful local ties.

Financed by Indian bankers, Arab Muslim slave traders had been sending African slaves to India from East and North Africa possibly as early as the fourth century. These Habshis—derived from the old name for Ethiopians (Abyssinians)—'were employed in very specialized jobs, as soldiers, palace guards, or bodyguards: they were able to rise through the ranks becoming generals, admirals and administrators.' They were specially sought after as warriors in the Deccan, as the Delhi Sultans had called a moratorium on the use of Turkish slaves in the south. So powerful did the African Malik Ambar become in the politics of Ahmednagar, for example, that Jahangir, the Mughal emperor who was directing his attention towards the Deccan, was piqued enough to refer to him in his memoirs as 'Ambar of dark fate' and 'that crafty, ill-starred one'.

By this time Raziya had been sultan for over three years, steadily consolidating her power. Unfortunately, her decision to promote Malik Yaqut backfired—by showing favour to a rank outsider, who was not even a Turk, it created an atmosphere of uncertainty at court to which the Turkish ghulams reacted in the way they often had, with violence and blood-letting.

The first one to rebel was Kabir Khan, who had earlier been pacified by the iqta of Lahore. Affronted by what he saw as Raziya's increasing autonomy, Kabir Khan rose in revolt in Lahore, five hundred kilometres away. Faced with this betrayal, Raziya refused to make any more concessions and, in 1239, she rode to Lahore at the head of the imperial army comprising Turks, Indians and Persians, all unquestioningly following their leader against a powerful fellow ghulam, an erstwhile brother of the band. She confronted him at the Chenab River, another hundred kilometres further. Crushed on one side by Raziya's army and on the other by the threatening hordes of Genghis Khan, Kabir Khan yielded to his sultan.

The amirs and ghulams now organized a more extensive revolt. Raziya was lured out of Delhi, where she was enormously popular, by a general uprising at Tabarhindh (in modern-day Bathinda, Punjab). The amir of Tabarhindh, Altunia, had been conspiring with Aytegin, the amir-hajib at the court of Delhi. When Raziya marched out, Yaqut, who had been left behind in Delhi, was seized by the rioters and killed. Raziya herself was overpowered at Tabarhindh and imprisoned in the fort.

In the end, Raziya was undone by the game of careful brinkmanship she attempted. She was betrayed by the very men she had earlier promoted in a bid to win their loyalty—Aytegin and Altunia. After they had her imprisoned, the amirs enthroned her half-brother Muizz al-Din Bahram Shah as sultan, but only after he had agreed to the creation of the new post of 'viceroy' for the amir-hajib, Aytegin. To further secure his imperial ambitions, Aytegin married Bahram Shah's sister, much as Iltutmish had done by marrying Qutb ud-Din's daughter. Bahram Shah, however, was not unaware of these manoeuvres and he eventually had Aytegin captured and killed. Altunia, now finding himself without his main ally, unexpectedly had Raziya released and married her. This marriage was a pragmatic transaction between Altunia and Raziya—he gained an ally to replace the one he'd lost and

Raziya got another chance to reclaim the throne of her father.

Despite her months of incarceration at Tabarhindh, Raziya was quick to realize that this would be her last chance to reclaim the throne of Delhi and was able to raise a considerable force that included Hindu Khokkars from Punjab, Jats and other tribes, as well as some amirs (who were still loyal) and Turks and mercenaries. Together with Altunia, Raziya marched to Delhi to confront her half-brother, the pretender to the throne, Bahram Shah. In this battle, led by Bahram himself, Raziya's army was routed, the Hindu soldiers deserted, and the surviving members scattered through the countryside. Raziya and Altunia were able to escape but were eventually overcome and killed while fleeing the neighbourhood of Kaithal in modern-day Haryana.

It is fitting that Raziya died as she had lived, fighting to regain what she saw as her lost inheritance, a warrior daughter of a slave king.

Amir Khusro, the Sufi poet and scholar, born half a century after Raziya, wrote of her:

> For three years in which her hand was strong
> No one laid a finger on one of her orders.
> In the fourth, since the page had turned from her matters
> The pen of fate drew a line through her.

Raziya's only true contemporary chronicler, Juzjani, writes generously of her talents:

> She was a great sovereign and sagacious, just, beneficent, the patron of the learned, a dispenser of justice, the cherisher of her subjects, and of warlike talent, and was endowed with all the admirable attributes and qualifications necessary for kings: but as she did not attain the destiny, in her creation, of being computed among men, of what advantage were all these excellent qualifications unto her?

Peter Jackson has shown that there was a fortuitous confluence of circumstances at the beginning of the Delhi Sultanate that made it easier for a woman to be respected in a position of authority. The nomadic background of the Turkish ghulams, especially those from the Pontic and Caspian steppes, meant that they were used to seeing women assume a more public role. Some of the ghulams were of Khitan or Qara-Khitan stock, Mongol-type pagan converts to Islam who founded dynasties in Turkestan. They would have had the example of Koyunk Khatun, a twelfth-century daughter of a Khitan leader, who ruled Turkestan after the death of her father. The Turk ghulams of the Sultanate, many of them first generation converts from the pagan steppes, never appeared to resent her gender. Indeed, Raziya's brothers Rukn al-Din and Bahram Shah were deposed much more quickly than Raziya was when they challenged the power of the ghulams. Raziya herself seemed to have regarded her gender as no hindrance and discarded purdah when it got in the way of her governing her kingdom. Though we cannot claim with certainty that Iltutmish intended her to rule after him, it is certain that she received the same education as her brothers growing up, as her talents and skill demonstrate.

But if Raziya and her contemporaries had a gallant disregard for her gender, the same was not true of future generations. Isami was the first to write about her reign in more gender-driven terms: 'I am told that she came out of purdah suddenly, discarded her modesty and became jovial.' In case his insinuation at slighting her is not clear, Isami further adds, 'everyone high and low used to enjoy the sight of her face.' And finally Isami concludes with a rambling diatribe on the many failings of women, from the appalling ('when the passions of a pious woman are inflamed, she concedes to an intimacy even with a dog') to the more specific ('to wear the crown, and fill the throne of kings, does not benefit a woman: this is the role exclusively meant for the experienced type of man').

One could argue that Isami was writing in the fourteenth

century, but the legacy of Raziya even in the twenty-first century has not fared much better. As recently as 2015, a TV series called *Razia Sultan*, purporting to be a historical drama, sabotaged the memory of a remarkable woman and turned it into an over-wrought and sensational love triangle between a scheming outsider, Yaqut, and a jealous and 'rakish' childhood love, Altunia. The show advertises Raziya as 'a lively, bright-eyed princess with no big aspirations. Just a curious little girl who grew up seeking answers... She loved her father Iltutmish the most'.

She was the daughter of a king, but Raziya, after an initial period of relying on her father's legacy, then actively distanced herself from Iltutmish and ruled unaided by any man. She became the sultan, ruling with her own titles—a remarkable achievement for a Muslim woman in the medieval world at a time when her female contemporaries in Europe, for instance, influenced by the Roman Catholic Church, were confined within the walls of their homes and kept out of all spheres of influence. The very few women of any political consequence at all were regents of their sons, or exceptions like Joan of Arc.

When Minhaj-i-Siraj Juzjani tabled the long list of rulers in Iltutmish's dynasty, he did Raziya the great honour of crediting her as the only war-leader—a Lashgarkash.

SEVEN

~

BEGUM HAZRAT MAHAL

RUDRANGSHU MUKHERJEE

Hazrat Mahal played an important role in the revolt against British rule in 1857. Married to the nawab of Awadh, Wajid Ali Shah, she came to power when the nawab was exiled and her twelve-year-old son was put on the throne in 1856. In this excerpt, Rudrangshu Mukherjee elaborates how Begum Hazrat Mahal became a leader of the people.

On 30 May, the mutiny reached Lucknow, the capital of Awadh, a kingdom that had been annexed by Lord Dalhousie in February 1856. That evening, an *emeute* occurred in Lucknow. This was an event waiting to happen. Kaye, who wrote a very early and detailed account of the uprising (he called it the 'Sepoy War') noted that the sepoys in the Lucknow cantonment had been in an 'uncertain state of semi-mutiny' waiting for events to develop 'sufficiently... elsewhere to encourage a general rising of the troops at Lucknow.' There had been enough signs that people in Lucknow were tense and anxious since early May when the 7th Regiment of the Awadh Irregular Infantry refused to accept the new cartridges that had been furnished to them. In the days immediately after the fall of Delhi, proclamations in Hindi, Urdu and Persian were put up all over the city calling upon the populace—both Hindus and Muslims—to unite, rise and kill the *firangis*. People began to display their hatred for the white man by carrying out acts of symbolic violence: figures were dressed up as Europeans and their heads were cut off in public places, much to the amusement and appreciation of the crowd that gathered. Such acts, as studies of popular unrest have shown, frequently occur in, or precede, episodes of insurgency.

To understand this popular anger against the firangi, it is necessary to place the uprising in Lucknow and the rest of Awadh in its historical context. Awadh was one of the earliest successor states of the Mughal Empire; as the latter declined as a centralizing force under a series of incompetent rulers, powerful noblemen began to carve out territories for themselves. In 1722, an important Mughal nobleman, Saadat Khan, refused the imperial order transferring him to Malwa and declared himself the independent ruler of Awadh based in Lucknow. Since then, Awadh had been a sprawling principality flourishing in the heart of north India. The word 'flourishing' is used advisedly. Muzaffar Alam has shown that Awadh was one of the areas where economic growth was noticeable within the overall decline of the Mughal Empire in the eighteenth century. Awadh's first brush with the English East India Company and therefore with British rule was at the battle of Baksar in October 1764, when the then Nawab of Awadh, Shuja-ud-Daula, joined forces with the Mughal Emperor, Shah Alam, and the Nawab of Bengal, Mir Qasim, to form a tripartite alliance against the British. Defeat at Baksar made Shuja-ud-Daula accept the terms set by the British, which included permission to the Company to trade in Awadh, agree to pay a subsidy to the British, ostensibly for the maintenance of a garrison of British troops for his 'protection', and have the presence in his court of a British Resident. Thus began a relationship that was one sided in favour of the British. Awadh, as one historian has pithily put it, became increasingly important not for what it could do, but for what it had to offer. This relationship and British trade sapped Awadh of its economic resources, and the growth of the trade and its changing nature served as the context for the truncation of the nawab's territory by Lord Wellesley in 1801.

Through the Resident, the British also established control over the administration and reduced the nawab (called a king by the British from 1819) into a figurehead. The situation was summed up by the historian Thomas Metcalf thus:

> With the subsidiary alliance drawn tightly about him, he could not ignore the British and act as before. But he had neither the training nor the military force to act upon the injunction of his European advisers. So the Nawabs who succeeded Saadat Ali Khan (post 1814), one after the other, increasingly abandoned the attempt to govern and retired into the *zanana*, where they amused themselves with wine, women and poetry. The sensuous life... did not reflect sheer perversity or weakness of character on the part of the Nawabs. Indolence was rather the only appropriate response to the situation in which the princes of Oudh were placed: in which they could not be overthrown but could not act effectively in either the old way or the new.

Metcalf also notes that this plight of the nawabs was pointed out by some British officers, like F.J. Shore and Henry Lawrence. This enforced inability to rule was interpreted by most British officials, especially Lord Dalhousie, as incompetence and a refusal to rule. Using misgovernment as a pretext, Dalhousie annexed Awadh on 7 February 1856 and sent the king Wajid Ali Shah to exile in Calcutta.

The annexation and the treatment meted out to Wajid Ali Shah caused an emotional upheaval in Lucknow and the countryside of Awadh. Having condemned Wajid Ali Shah as an incompetent ruler, the British had not quite reckoned with the fact that he was a popular king, much loved by his subjects. The annexation was resented: a folk song of the time lamented: *Angrez Bahadur ain: mulk lain linho* (the honourable English came and took the country). When Wajid Ali Shah left Lucknow for the last time to go to Calcutta, many of his subjects followed him all the way to Kanpur singing dirges. A contemporary wrote, 'The condition of this town [Lucknow] without any exaggeration was such that it appeared that on the departure of Jan-i Alam, the life was gone out of the body, and the body of this town had been left lifeless... there was no street or market and house which did not wail out the cry of agony in separation of Jan-i Alam.' A folk song of the period echoed the sentiments: 'Noble and peasant all wept together/ and all the world wept and wailed/ Alas! The chief has bidden adieu to/ his country and gone abroad.'

The land revenue policies the British adopted in Awadh caused a different kind of upheaval in the countryside. The Summary Settlement of 1856 was directed against the *taluqdars*, who held real power in the rural world as large landholders with forts and retainers. British land revenue policy considered taluqdars as interlopers who stood between the government and the peasants. The British destroyed many of the forts and through the Summary Settlement dispossessed the taluqdars of large parts of their landholding. The Summary Settlement halved the holdings of the taluqdars. Furthermore, in many of the districts the land revenue assessment was pitched higher than it had been in nawabi times. The reverberations of these developments in rural Awadh and the exile of the king were felt keenly in the sepoy lines, as most of the sepoys of the Bengal Army came from southern Awadh. This entire amalgam of interrelated issues was communicated to Captain Barrow by Hanwant Singh, who had provided him protection during the uprising. When the latter was sending Barrow off to Allahabad, Hanwant Singh told him: 'Sahib, your countrymen came into this country and drove out our king. You sent your officers round the districts to examine the titles to the estates. At one blow you took from me lands which from time immemorial had been in my family. I submitted. Suddenly misfortune fell upon you. The people of the land rose against you. You came to me whom you had despoiled. I have saved you. But now—now I march at the head of my retainers to Lakhnao to try and drive you out of the country.'

This context helps to understand what happened in Lucknow after the mutiny erupted. Henry Lawrence had expressed his anxiety about the districts of Awadh. As things unfolded there, there was a replay of what had happened after the fall of Delhi and the transmission of the news. The cantonments in the districts had been waiting for the developments in Lucknow. Once the Lucknow garrison had raised the flag of mutiny, the other cantonments followed in quick succession: Sitapur, Faizabad, Gonda-Bharaich, Sultanpur and Salon. The fall of one station, since it signalled the weakness—and even the fall—of British power, contributed to the rising of another garrison. After they had mutinied, the sepoys, the villagers, the taluqdars and their retainers marched to Lucknow exactly as Hanwant Singh had told Barrow. By the end of June, a large rebel army—7000 to 8000 strong—was ready to descend on Lucknow, where, under the orders of Henry Lawrence, the entire British population had taken refuge in the Residency. The inevitable military encounter—the first between the British and the rebels—took place on the last day of June at Chinhat. The British were defeated and had to retreat. The news of the loss had an electrifying impact in Lucknow and in other parts of Awadh. It was taken as a fact that British rule had 'past [sic] away forever and the "Nawabee" is restored as a matter of course.' The siege of the Residency commenced, and the victory was celebrated with groups of rebels going round the streets of Lucknow chanting 'Bom Mahadeo'. Away from the streets and the people, steps were taken to bring back and establish the political order that had existed before the annexation. It was not possible to bring back Wajid Ali Shah, so powerful taluqdars and former ministers conferred and decided to put Wajid Ali Shah's twelve-year-old son, Birjis Qadr, on the throne on 5 July. The rebels embraced the new king. 'You are Kanahaiya [Krishna],' they said. It was during the preparations for the coronation that Hazrat Mahal made her entry into the annals of the uprising and thus on the stage of history.

Who was Hazrat Mahal apart from being the mother of the new king and therefore the wife and the Begum of Wajid Ali Shah? This is where historians begin to tread on relatively unknown territory. Little is known about her. The scattered and often unconfirmed bits of evidence have been very carefully stitched together by the historian Rosie Llewellyn Jones. According to her, Hazrat Mahal came from a very humble background—her father was an African slave. She joined the Pari Khanna music school in Lucknow. Members of this school had Pari (fairy) suffixed to their names; thus, she was called Mahak Pari. Through her talents or good looks or both, she caught the eye and the fancy of Wajid Ali Shah, who made her into one of his many *muta* (temporary wives). In 1845, she gave birth to a son, and this led to her being elevated by Wajid Ali Shah to the position of Mahal (a title that Wajid Ali Shah gave to his better placed wives, according to Sharar) and she came to be styled Nawab Iftikhar un-Nisa Begum Hazrat Mahal Sahiba. In 1850, fortune stopped smiling on Hazrat Mahal. That year Wajid Ali Shah gave talaq to six wives, including Hazrat Mahal, who was dismissed from the harem. It was rumoured at the time that the king's mother, who wielded considerable influence over him, had persuaded him to disassociate himself from his wives who were of lowly origin. The divorce and the dismissal from the zanana meant that when Wajid Ali Shah was forced to leave Lucknow for Calcutta, Hazrat Mahal did not find a place in his entourage. It is also entirely possible that the talaq and the exit from the royal household implied that she had been stripped of her fancy title. She was officially no longer a begum. But through a quirk of fate, her son became the king and the *wali* (governor) of the Mughal Badshah and thus she regained her title of Begum. She became the power behind the throne in Awadh and all orders that emanated in the name of Birjis Qadr were hers. A rebellion of the people had made her a leader, and she became the leader of the people.

EIGHT

~

NUR JAHAN

RUBY LAL

Nur Jahan ruled the Mughal empire as chief consort of Emperor Jahangir from 1620–1627. She signed and issued orders and even led troops into battle. Narrating an episode where Nur Jahan took down a tiger in a single shot, Ruby Lal reflects on the new kind of power she wielded in the Mughal court.

In the autumn of 1619, when the days were clear and cool, perfect for travel, the royal cavalcade of Emperor Jahangir and Empress Nur Jahan, his twentieth and favorite wife, set out from Agra, the capital of Mughal India, headed for the Himalayan foothills. The people of Mathura, a popular pilgrimage site along the emperor's route, were anxious for his arrival. For months, a tiger had been attacking villagers and visitors, then disappearing into the forest, evading local hunters. No divine intervention seemed to be forthcoming from Lord Krishna and his consort Radha, the Hindu deities worshipped in Mathura's temples. But the emperor could solve the problem. Killing tigers had long been a royal prerogative.

Jahangir—his name meant Conqueror of the World in Persian, the language of the court—was the fourth of the Mughal emperors, a Muslim dynasty established by invasion early in the sixteenth century. Descendants of the Central Asian nomad kings Chingiz [Genghis] Khan and Tamerlane, the Mughals ruled much of Hindu-majority India for more than three hundred years.

According to one excited observer, the imperial procession included "fifteen hundred thousand" people—men, women, and children; courtiers, soldiers, and servants—along with ten thousand elephants and a great deal of artillery. The procession halted near Mathura, and attendants began erecting hundreds of magnificent tents, with the harem quarters marked with intricately carved red screens. While the traveling court was still being set up, a group of local huntsmen appeared and begged Jahangir to do something about the tiger.

Unfortunately, the emperor was obligated to decline. Several years before, Jahangir had taken a vow to give up hunting when he turned fifty. After that, he'd promised Allah, he would injure no living being with his own hands. He was two months past that milestone birthday, and had recently renewed the vow as an offering on behalf of a favorite four-year-old grandson, traveling with him, who suffered from epilepsy. Shooting a tiger was now out of the question for Jahangir. The empress, however, was there to protect her subjects.

Beautiful and accomplished, Nur Jahan was the daughter of nobles who'd fled persecution in Persia. She was also the widow of a court official implicated in a plot against Jahangir, but that didn't stop the emperor from falling hard for her. She was thirty-four when they married, nearly middle-aged in the Mughal world. Since their wedding in 1611, the same year that Shakespeare premiered *The Tempest*, Nur Jahan (Light of the World in Persian, the name bestowed by her husband), had proved to be a devoted wife, a wise and just queen, a shrewd politician—and an expert markswoman. Her shooting skills were already legendary.

A few years earlier, she'd amazed her husband and his courtiers by slaying four tigers with only six shots.

On October 23, 1619, Nur Jahan mounted an elephant and settled into the howdah, the elaborate litter on the animal's back, holding a musket. The mahout, the elephant handler, led her along the sandy track toward the forest. Nur Jahan accompanied her husband, Jahangir, on his own elephant, and they were followed by a long line of courtiers, some on superbly ornamented elephants and horses and others in red and gold jeweled palanquins with silken seats, decorated with garlands of flowers and carried by attendants. Portraits of Nur Jahan from the period suggest that she was wearing a regal turban, much like the ones favored by the emperor and distinguished noble men, but highly unusual for a woman; a knee-length tunic with a sash around the waist over tight trousers; and earrings and a necklace of rubies, diamonds, or pearls. Her shoes were open at the back, exposing the henna designs on her feet. At forty-two, she was still praised by her contemporaries for her luminous beauty.

Local hunters on foot guided the party past fields of barley, peas, and cotton, lush from the recent rains. Along the way, they spotted herds of cattle, goats, and blackbuck with long corkscrew horns. When they reached the forest, the emperor and empress could barely see beyond the dense wall of creepers, bushes, and trees—lofty *nim*, thorny *babul*, and many others. The hunters showed the empress and her retinue the spot where the tiger was likely to appear, and they waited.

Soon Nur's elephant, in the lead, began groaning and stepping nervously from side to side; the mahout couldn't make it stand still, and Nur Jahan's howdah lurched precariously. From his own elephant, Jahangir looked on, silent and focused. Later, he would recall the moment in the *Jahangirnama* (The memoirs of Jahangir), a journal he began when he ascended to the throne in 1605 that would serve as the public record of his reign. "An elephant is not at ease when it smells a tiger, and is continually in movement," he wrote, "and to hit with a gun from a litter is a very difficult matter."

The tiger emerged from the trees. Nur lifted her musket, aimed between the animal's eyes, and pulled the trigger. Despite the swaying of her elephant, one shot was enough; the tiger fell to the ground, killed instantly. Jahangir was delighted. A woman shooting publicly was rare; a woman shooting with such expertise was unheard-of.

Nur's shooting skill wasn't the only thing that made her highly unusual. She held a position in the empire never before filled by a woman: co-sovereign. For more than a decade and a half, from a few years after their wedding until Jahangir's death, Nur Jahan ruled along with her husband, effectively and prominently, successfully navigating the labyrinth of feudal courtly politics and the male-centered culture of the Mughal world. She issued her own imperial orders, and coins of the realm bore her name along with her husband's. In Islamic thought and practice, the edicts and the coins were convincing technical signs of sovereignty. Furthermore, Nur sat where no other Mughal queen had sat before or would after, in the *jharokha*, an elaborately carved balcony projecting from the palace wall, from which government business was conducted. Subjects gathered below the *jharokha* to pray for her health, and getting a look at her was considered auspicious. More important, nobles sometimes presented themselves below the imperial balcony "and listen[ed] to her dictates," according to a contemporary historian. "At last her authority reached such a pass that the King was such only in name . . . Repeatedly he gave out that he bestowed the sovereignty on Nur Jahan Begam."

A generation earlier, Jahangir's father, Akbar the Great, had ordered all royal women—wives, daughters, and concubines—to be sequestered behind harem walls. He called them "the veiled ones." But three decades after Akbar's dictate, Nur Jahan was on view in the most male and public of places. A new kind of power was on display.

NINE

~

THE MAHARANIS OF TRAVANCORE

MANU S. PILLAI

From the first regency in Travancore, established in 1810 with Rani Gowri Lakshmi Bayi's rule, to the coronation of Her Highness Maharajah Pooradam Tirunal, Manu S. Pillai describes the unique case of regencies in Travancore in this excerpt.

The role of a Regent in India was typically a limited one. He or she represented the monarch during the period of the latter's minority, and the Regency government was only an interim administration. In the conventional sense, while Regents could govern the realm, they were not permitted to make any significant changes in the laws or constitution of the country as sovereigns might; any new measures were to be consistent with the existing framework and of a nature that could be sustained when the rightful ruler came of age. Politically, what was perhaps most important was that Regents could not usually rule alone in colonial India; they were to head a Council of Regency, comprising eminent leaders of the land, usually nominated by the British after the latter were assured that they would not become impediments to the interests of the Raj. This was to safeguard that complete authority was not vested in one person during the minority of the monarch, which might be too tempting to give up when the time came. The Regent could preside over the temporary arrangements, but could certainly not become a dictator.

In the nineteenth century there had been a number of regencies in India, some of them quite noteworthy, such as of Begum Qudsia III in Bhopal, Sir Salar Jung in Hyderabad, and Sir T. Madhava Rao in Baroda. Normally, the Government of India preferred the Council of Regency to be headed by the mother of the minor prince or the senior consort of the preceding ruler. Thus, in Mysore from 1895 to 1902, for instance, the Dowager Maharani Vani Vilas Sannidhana held the position of Regent, and in the 1920s, Gwalior and Cooch Behar had two widows in power. However, these women were only figureheads whose role entailed ratifying the better judgements of their Councils of Regency. Dewans were the executive members on these bodies acting as the real rulers, requiring the Maharanis simply to sanction their resolutions. Most often, these dependent women had no other option but to comply. In Mysore, for example, the minister was told to consult the Maharani only 'as is practicable and desirable' and otherwise liaise directly with the Government of India, by now relocated from Calcutta to Delhi. In other words, the Maharanis were titular heads of state, only lending royal legitimacy to the Acts issued by the Councils that really controlled interim power.

The case of Travancore, however, was exceptional. The defining aspect here was that female members of the dynasty were inherently entitled to their positions due to the matrilineal system, and did not owe their status to the accident of marriage. As sisters of the Rajahs, they carried in them the same royal blood, and were entitled to rule whenever eligible males heirs were found wanting. 'The position of [the] woman in [Kerala],' wrote

K.P. Padmanabha Menon, 'is altogether different from that of her sister [elsewhere in India]. She is practically mistress of the house, whether as mother or sister of the [senior male member]. She has a recognised legal position. The principle of [Malayali] law is that the whole [estate] property belongs to her and the [senior male] is simply the manager on her behalf … Her general education is on a par with her brothers, and her intellectual capacity in the matter of special studies is in no way inferior. There have been and there are ladies of remarkable attainments in [Kerala].' Thus when Queen Ashure reigned over Travancore in the seventeenth century during a minority, she did so as an absolute and supreme monarch. Later historians would refer to her as a Regent, but neither this term nor office existed in the political vocabulary of her day. By the nineteenth century, however, the concept of Regency had arrived in the state through the medium of the English East India Company, which had acquired the right to intervene in all matters concerning Travancore, including the line of succession.

It was in 1810 that Rani Gowri Lakshmi Bayi commenced her rule when there were no male members at all in the royal house. She was recognised as sovereign, but the times were unusually turbulent and Travancore was in the midst of grave internal and external crises. There had been mutinies and rebellions within that threatened the dynasty, even as the Company was becoming disconcertingly aggressive outside, annexing states and deposing rulers at the drop of a proverbial hat. Their attitude towards women also influenced matters in that the authorities could not see how a young girl of twenty could possibly manage so many difficulties in Travancore—up to the late eighteenth century, women were seen in Europe as private property, with little freedom, no rights of inheritance, and wife battering was considered legitimate domestic behaviour. In essence, the female, when it came to intelligent, worldly affairs, had ineluctably to submit to the will of men. So Gowri Lakshmi Bayi, as a woman, found herself unable to claim the confidence of the British, palled perpetually therefore by the threat of expulsion.

The one thing that could secure the throne to her dynasty at this critical time when colonial chauvinists pulled the political strings was the birth of a male heir, whom the Company would recognise. For until that boy were given a chance to rule, they could be counted upon not to annexe the state. Unsurprisingly, then, when in 1813 the Rani gave birth to a son, she was asked to 'step down' from the throne, install him there, and govern hereafter as Regent. In the interests of expediency and security, she did exactly that, and with this we find the first 'Regency' arising in Travancore. However, what is most vital here is that although she took the title of Regent, Gowri Lakshmi Bayi did not surrender any real powers. While the Sword of State was placed in the hands of the baby boy, she continued as interim monarch with unrestrained actual authority. All legislative Acts were issued in her name, for instance, and not in his as would be the case with normal regencies. When she died in 1814, her sister Gowri Parvathi Bayi took over as Regent, and continued to exercise full powers. The highest currency of the land carried her insignia, and when durbars were held, it was she who occupied the throne. Indeed, during his minority, the boy who was supposedly the real monarch, never even sat in her presence. As the Resident noted at the time, 'the people were accustomed to regard her with the reverence and respect which they paid to their Rajahs' and saw her 'occupy the place of the Rajah and scarcely found any difference in the constitution of the state'. Both these women, therefore, were Regents only in name. Locally, they were treated as sovereign, with all the attendant authority, and this would define Sethu Lakshmi Bayi's position also a century afterwards.

A few days after Mulam Tirunal's death, the incumbent Resident, Mr C.W.E. Cotton, called on the Rani to discuss her Regency government and other imminent affairs. For all her previous trepidation and reluctance with regard to ruling, Sethu

Lakshmi Bayi now, when it came to it, more than rose to the occasion. She pointed out her anomalous position in Travancore, citing that as per matrilineal law, she was now the head of the family and ought to rule in her own name and right. Just because Gowri Lakshmi Bayi, for reasons of political pragmatism, had acquiesced in an inferior title, it was not fair to expect the same from her. Sethu Lakshmi Bayi was technically correct, and some years ago the High Court in Trivandrum had accepted that when 'a senior female takes up the management [of the family] during the minority of the male members, she does not take it up on behalf of the eldest minor male member but in her own right'. Mr Cotton also accepted that while normally the senior female of the family had 'unrestricted powers' during a minority, in the royal family 'the strict letter of this law was modified in 1813' by Gowri Lakshmi Bayi. By doing so, that Rani created a *new* precedent, namely of Regency, which was followed without question by Gowri Parvathi Bayi after her. Additionally, when Mulam Tirunal wrote to the Viceroy in 1917, he too referred to the eligibility of the senior female as Regent and not as sovereign ruler. So, this new tradition, though acknowledged as an invention of colonial jurisprudence and political circumstances, had to be complied with uncomplainingly, and taken to be immutable.

That said, however, the Government of India did concede to Sethu Lakshmi Bayi the rights previous Rani-Regents had enjoyed. They confirmed that 'her powers will be unrestricted as Regent' and locally she would enjoy the status of a monarch. And this was ensured by the concession that there would be no Council of Regency in the state, vesting complete and autocratic control in the hands of the Rani. But there were some ceremonial deprivations. So, while the Legislative Council pledged allegiance to Sethu Lakshmi Bayi, and not the minor prince, the Rani could not sit on the throne; she had to make do with a 'Regent's Chair'. Similarly, while she would enjoy the position of monarch locally with all attendant honours, if British Governors or Viceroys visited, she would have to step back and accord precedence to the young boy. In that sense, the custom of Gowri Parvathi Bayi, which was the model emulated, was not followed to the letter. But Sethu Lakshmi Bayi did not press the matter and accepted her titular demotion as Regent insofar as it entailed no actual demotion of authority.

Once this was settled, the durbar astrologers were summoned to determine the dates for the installation of the new Maharajah and the Regent. On 20 August 1924, the Junior Rani's son performed the relevant ceremonies and took charge of the Sword of State before the shrine of Sri Padmanabhaswamy. Then came the turn of Sethu Lakshmi Bayi. Again, since in Travancore the Regent's was not merely an administrative office but a de facto monarchy, she too had to go through exactly the same religious rituals as the boy, with the exception that flowers and prasadam replaced the Sword of State. On 1 September the Rani ascended the Sreemukha Mandapam in the temple and was invested with the right to govern Travancore. As with the rulers before her, Sethu Lakshmi Bayi proceeded from the temple to the Chokkatta Mandapam in the fort, wherefrom she gave her first (customary) orders to the Dewan, commanding him to ensure the correct and meticulous management of all the temples in the country. Presents were distributed to an assembly of Brahmins and the principal ceremony was concluded. She returned, then, not to Moonbeam but to Anantha Vilasam in the Valiya Kottaram complex of the Maharajahs, which was to be her official residence now. A large crowd of people waited there to pay their respects, carrying with them the *nuzzer* or *tirumulkazhcha* that was usually offered to the ruler at an audience. But Sethu Lakshmi Bayi decided to end the custom; the Dewan was ordered to let it be known that the Rani did not want any presents to be offered by her subjects who wished to greet her, opening her reign on a positive note.

That afternoon an official durbar was convened to install the minor prince and the Regent. The soldiers of Travancore's nominal army (as permitted by the British) called the Nair Brigade and the Royal Bodyguard having taken their positions, at 3:45 p.m. the Junior Rani, her younger son, the new Elayarajah, and daughter arrived. The Dewan received and led them in, following which at 3:50 Sethu Lakshmi Bayi drove in a state carriage drawn by four white horses, to the resounding boom of a twenty-one-gun salute. Chithira Tirunal, the minor Maharajah, arrived in similar circumstances at 3:55, after whom the Resident, decked with his many medals and in complete formal uniform, made his appearance at 4.00 p.m. After a preliminary speech, Mr Cotton led the young boy to the Ivory Throne and handed him 'a turban plumed with the drooping feathers of the bird of paradise, held in place by an aigrette of diamonds and emeralds and two large pendant pearls'. Thereafter, Sethu Lakshmi Bayi took her seat on the right side of the throne, in the ornate Regent's Chair, and the installation proclamation was read out to all seated in court; the Rani had again broken with tradition and for the first time allowed those present to take a seat in the presence of the royal family.

Once the proclamation was rendered, the dignitaries, including Chithira Tirunal and Sethu Lakshmi Bayi, moved to the balcony outside. There, Mr Raghavaiah read out the proclamation once again, and another twenty-one-gun salute heralded the inauguration of the new regime. On their return to the hall, Mr Cotton delivered a speech, announcing at the end that both the Ranis of Travancore would henceforward be styled, at the orders of the Viceroy, as *Maharanis*. This came as a general surprise and was received with thunderously loyal applause from the assembled nobility and officialdom. The Resident's speech was followed by Sethu Lakshmi Bayi's inaugural address—a neat, regular affair, lamenting first the demise of Mulam Tirunal, pledging loyalty to the British Crown, and expressing the hope that she would be able to 'acquit myself of my new duties conscientiously and without passion or prejudice'. With that the durbar came to a conclusion and the Resident departed first, followed by the royal family and the other distinguished persons gathered.

In all this what was perhaps most fascinating was Sethu Lakshmi Bayi's new status as interim ruler. While the Government of India imposed the inferior title of Regent on her, traditionally within the state she was always heralded in a distinctive manner. For one, unlike administrative Regents, she had an elaborate regnal title, equal to that of a male sovereign. However, there was more. In popular parlance she would be the Maharani Regent or the Senior Maharani, similar to her female counterparts in other states. But what was distinct was that in all official documents and proclamations, she held the title of Pooradam Tirunal Maharajah. In fact even the Resident had addressed her as Maharajah in his proclamation. This was unprecedented in India, just as the status of the Attingal Rani was also unique. For under the matrilineal system, where the sexes were equal, the monarch's gender was of little consequence. It was the position and its dignity that mattered and whoever exercised supreme authority in the state and in the royal house was held to be the Maharajah. The Government of India, with its Western outlook and cultural constraints, might have called it a Regency. But to the local people of Travancore, the reign of Mulam Tirunal Maharajah was rightfully succeeded by that of Pooradam Tirunal Maharajah, just as it would one day be relinquished to Chithira Tirunal Maharajah. To the Government of India, thus, the young lady just installed was the Maharani Regent. But to the masses, she was Her Highness Maharajah Pooradam Tirunal of Travancore.

TEN

~

PRINCESS SANATOMBI

BINODINI

Translated from the Manipuri by L. Somi Roy

Binodini wrote The Princess and the Political Agent *(originally* Boro Saheb Ongbi Sanatombi*) based on the life of her aunt, Princess Sanatombi of Manipur. The novel narrates the love story of Sanatombi, a Meitei princess, and the British representative Lt Col. Henry P. Maxwell. This excerpt recounts Sanatombi's early rebellions in the palace.*

Sanatombi saw Manipur's last war first-hand. She witnessed as a young child the bitter rivalries of the princes, their quarrels, the entanglements of politics. She had seen it all: the fears, the sorrows, the consultations, the talks.

And there were many internal matters of the palace. She saw the splendid throne her grandfather his lordship Chandrakirti sat on for thirty-six years. But she did not get to live in the palace for very long. She was given in marriage at a young age to a man called Manikchand from the Nongmaithem family. There was a reason for this.

One day the Grand Queen Mother summoned Jasumati, consort of her royal grandson Crown Prince Surchandra and said, 'My dear, keep a close eye on your daughter. She is wilful and is going to be a handful. It is not enough to be kind-hearted. It will not do to be an accommodating and accepting worm of a person. You do not have any male offspring. The astrologers also say your daughter is of strong birth. I want to find a good match for her and get her married. What do you think?'

'The Grand Queen Mother needs only to instruct us. What can your humble servant say? After you inform your royal grandson, I defer to whatever the Divine Majesty and the Grand Queen Mother decide,' replied the meek Lady of Satpam.

Jasumati was a gentle woman. No one in the palace talked about her much. She may have had her disappointments and sorrows but she expressed them to no one. Most people in the palace did not even know of her existence. Her senior sister-wife Premamayi, Lady of Ngangbam, dominated all. Even though Premamayi was not the first wife of Surchandra, she overshadowed all—and so it must be. It was only to be expected that the clever rises above the many. It might be said that Jasumati merely gave birth to her daughter, for Sanatombi spent most of her time with her co-mother the Lady of Ngangbam, and the Grand Queen Mother. She only came home to sleep and her mother barely got to see her at all. She spent her days going from one household in the palace to another. Jasumati worried about her too. She knew her daughter was unruly, strong-willed and driven to win. It would have been better if she had been a boy, she thought to herself. Time and again Sanatombi would cause an uproar and stir up trouble. Even when as a mother she could not bear it any longer she could not beat Sanatombi or discipline her, for the Grand Queen Mother stood as her bulwark. The Grand Queen Mother, Lady of Meisnam, doted excessively on her great-grandchild. And then she says—Watch your daughter closely, when it is she who allows her to run wild...—but who could she have said this to? There was no one who could dare to talk back to the Grand Queen Mother, the Lady of Meisnam. So, even though she followed all palace protocol with great care, she suffered defeat at the hands of Sanatombi; she weakened when it came to her. Her great-grandmother favoured the unruly Sanatombi.

∽

One day when Sanatombi had grown up a bit, she said, 'I will play kang, Grand Queen Mother.' 'Of course, my grandchild shall play. And who will be the kang teams?' The Grand Queen Mother arranged it all. The court shuffleboard teams were Hijam Leikai and the palace. They gathered only the prettiest girls among them, both the palace and Hijam Leikai. They established many rules—no borrowing of pucks, no throwing of pucks in the air, and suchlike. The shuffleboard court was polished with fresh milk. There was a lot of noisy activity. Sanatombi was going to play her first game of court shuffleboard at the palace. But as the sorry tale unspooled, Sanatombi came to her royal great-grandmother, her face red with fury, and demanded, 'Grand Queen Mother, beat Lukhoi. He has stopped us from playing kang, he says we cannot play.'

A little while later, there was a great hue and cry. 'Sanatombi has bitten Prince Lukhoi! Oh no, what is to be done!'

The matter was this. Prince Lukhoi had barred Sanatombi when she arrived to play at the shuffleboard court. Lukhoi was born to the Lady of Ngangbam, wife of Surchandra. The Lady of Ngangbam was not only clever but she had even produced a male offspring, and one day, sooner or later, Lukhoi could ascend the throne at Kangla. Even though he was a child, Lukhoi was well aware of this. His unthinking caregivers and attendants never failed to remind the child of it, and so he was very headstrong. He and Sanatombi were not that far apart in age.

He had come in while Sanatombi and her friends were

noisily busy in the shuffleboard court and said, 'Is it true you all are going to play kang, Royal Elder Sister? You may not play.'

'Why not?'

'Because I am telling you. You cannot.'

'And who are you? Should I stop just because you do not allow it? It is none of your business. I am doing it. What are you going to do about it?'

'You cannot do as you like.'

'And why not?'

'I am Prince Lukhoi.'

'And I am Sanatombi.'

'I am the male offspring—you are female.'

'What attitude, Mr Male Offspring!'

Sanatombi flared up in anger. It was true she was a daughter. A daughter had no claim upon the throne at Kangla. But she did not accept this; she did not accept being told she could not do as she wanted. She did not know that her mother who only had daughters was not considered a blessed woman. It was especially true in the palace. How was she any different from a barren woman? Her birth mother lived choked in secret, her throat constricted, dry. It was not as if Sanatombi had not sometimes heard her mother heave a deep sigh. But she never found out why. The Grand Queen Mother had never once said to her face, 'You are a female; you are of inferior destiny.' She had said, 'Now, there's my great-granddaughter, now that's my great-granddaughter.' But sometimes late at night, her mother Jasumati said to her quietly, 'Sanatombi, you are a daughter, so conduct yourself with that knowledge... ... .' What was it she said? Sanatombi, her thoughts wandering somewhere else, paid her scant heed. Lukhoi not allowing her to play court shuffleboard enraged Sanatombi no end.

Sanatombi said, 'So what if you are a male?'

'I am stopping you from playing kang, that's what,' Lukhoi answered with attitude. He was also just a boy at the time. It was around that age just before youth when boys are at their most obnoxious.

Sanatombi said, 'What is it that you want?'

'Let Hijam Ibemhal play on the palace team.'

'Oh really? The one from Hijam Leikai?'

'Even so.'

'Oh, is that why you are coming and sticking your nose in?'

'Why did you go to Grand Queen Mother without telling me first you were playing kang?'

'Meaning?'

'You have to inform me first—I was going to rehearse my dance here. If you want to play kang here, you have to inform me first.'

'Your dancing goes on in the women dancers' court. Has this male offspring no shame, being in the women dancers' court?'

'Men should be part of the women dancers' court. You cannot play kang, and that is that.' Saying this, he plunked himself down cross-legged in the middle of the shuffleboard court. Smoothened and polished for many days beforehand, the shuffleboard court shone like a mirror. It was not to be stepped upon. Sanatombi could not bear it any longer. She leapt at him and grabbed his hair. The two fought, they could not be pulled apart.

Suddenly Lukhoi yelled, 'She bit me! The witch, the witch!'

Sanatombi went off to tell the Grand Queen Mother. Lukhoi was left crying, yelling 'She-Demon, She-Demon' at her. 'She-Demon' was Sanatombi's hated nickname.

All hurried towards the quarters of the Grand Queen Mother, Sanatombi's mother, the Lady of Satpam, heard and came running. She lashed out at her child and hit her. She struck out at her wildly. Sanatombi did not cry. She stood rock still. The others separated them. Hearing of this, Sanatombi's nurse came running and put her arms around her child.

Sanatombi said, 'Of course, I beat him up. Can he do as he

pleases just because he's a male offspring? I will beat him, I will keep on beating him.'

'Look at the mouth on her.' Her mother tried to hit her again. The Grand Queen Mother tried to separate them. Then Sanatombi went and stood by the Grand Queen Mother, watching. She was very pleased with herself.

Lukhoi's mother, the Lady of Ngangbam, arrived. Laughing, she said, 'Do not beat her, sister-wife. Why make a big thing of a matter between children?' Saying this, she examined her child's wounds. She did not mean what she said, for she was upset.

'Please do as you see fit, elder sister-wife. I am not going to be able to handle this girl. Look how she has bitten the child on his arm... Here, let Mother take a look.'

The Lady of Ngangbam laughed and said, 'Of course you should beat him, my child. How can he be disrespectful to his older royal sister? Lukhoi, say you are sorry to your older sister. Why did you try to destroy my daughter's kang court? What right does a boy have to do that.' She pretended to blame her son.

'Why should I kowtow when I did no wrong?'

'How he lies and says he did no wrong!'

They went at each other again. The Lady of Ngangbam stopped them, laughing. They made light of the matter but both the Lady of Ngangbam and the Lady of Satpam each knew what the other was thinking.

There were countless incidents and uproars like this because of Sanatombi. The girl-bearing Jasmati conducted herself with great discretion. But male offspring or female did not matter to Sanatombi. She did as she pleased. Controlling her was a major headache for Jasumati.

ELEVEN

~

A PRINCESS REMEMBERS

GAYATRI DEVI

Maharani Gayatri Devi was the third wife of Maharaja Sawai Man Singh II of Jaipur. Following India's independence, she became a successful politician of the Swatantra Party. This excerpt, from her memoir A Princess Remembers, *describes the 1962 Lok Sabha election in which she won 192,909 out of 246,516 votes cast, one of the biggest electoral landslides the world has seen.*

In 1962 the Swatantra Party was contesting elections for the first time. There was a meeting of some of its leaders and prominent party members in Jaipur, and there it was decided that besides contesting the Jaipur parliamentary seat myself, I should be responsible for securing the election of candidates for the whole area that had been the old state of Jaipur. This was a serious responsibility for someone without political experience. Jaipur state covered about 16,000 square miles. It had five parliamentary seats, and forty seats in the State Legislative Assembly of Rajasthan. Finding suitable candidates immediately presented a great problem. The Swatantra was a new party, and besides, many of the eminent citizens we approached refused to stand for an opposition party for fear of government pressure and reprisals. Businessmen were worried that their import permits might be cancelled or supplies of essential materials might be delayed. We did eventually manage to attract a number of good candidates, but through all the preliminary work I was continually confronted with evidences of my own ignorance of how much had to be done before a political campaign could be launched. I had never before heard of electoral rolls, did not know the names of the different constituencies, and did not realize that there were special seats reserved for the Harijans and the tribal people. I knew nothing about election agents, nominations, withdrawals, or parliamentary boards. Very fortunately, I had expert advisers and assistants from the party, the Thakur of Dudu, one of Jai's most loyal jagirdars and an election agent with a team of tireless workers who all performed magnificently—in educating me as much as in organizing the campaign. The President of the Swatantra party in Rajasthan, the Maharawal Dungarpur and the Vice President, the Raja of Bhinai gave me guidance and advice.

As soon as it was known that I was actually running for Parliament, people from all sorts of different sections of society kept coming to Rajmahal to ask Jai and other members of our family to stand as candidates. Jai made up his mind to stay out of politics and couldn't be persuaded to change it, but both Joey and Pat were roped in. Joey as a candidate for the State Legislative Assembly from a constituency where he would be opposing the Home Minister of Rajasthan and Pat, at the last minute, as the parliamentary candidate from the Dausa constituency that held the first capital of Jai's ancestors.

This seat was to have been contested by the General Secretary of the Swatantra Party, but he decided that he would be more useful touring the country before the elections and entering Parliament later in a by-election. Minoo Masani left it to Jai to find a replacement. Jai went to the constituency, and asked the people whom they would like as a candidate. He suggested a number of possibilities—lawyers and eminent public men—but the people insisted that he should stand himself and failing that, that he should propose a member of his own family. There was no question of Bubbles standing for election, as he was in the army. Joey was already committed, so there remained only Pat, who was eligible as he had just turned 25 and was working in Calcutta.

That morning I telephoned Pat to ask if he would agree to stand if Jai was unable to persuade the people to accept any other candidate. He was very reluctant about the whole thing, explaining that he would have no time to campaign and even if he were elected, would hardly be able to fulfil his commitments to his constituents in Jaipur when his own work would keep him in Calcutta. I assured him that his father would not put forward his name unless it was absolutely necessary. We waited impatiently for Jai to come back; it was well past midnight when his cavalcade arrived. Exhausted and covered with dust, Jai came upstairs and said simply, "I'm afraid it's Pat."

We telephoned him again the next morning, and he was furious, saying that he couldn't possibly campaign for more than ten days. We tried to calm him down and urged him to come to Jaipur at once, because the nominations were to be closed at 3 p.m. three days later. Pat said he would fly to Delhi and motor from there, but lunchtime on the last day he still hadn't arrived, and we were all waiting anxiously on the front terrace of Rajmahal. Telephones kept ringing as the press and well-wishers asked for news of his arrival. At 2:30 he drove up, scarcely said "hello" before he hurried to the Collectorate to file his nomination just before the books were closed and then disappeared again, to return only for the last fortnight of the campaign.

Once we had managed to find candidates for all the seats, the campaign began in earnest. To start off, Jai came with me to Sheikhawati, a part of Jaipur state. It was a desert region, starved for water, where the very scanty irrigation enables the people even in the best of times, to grow only one crop a year. Many of the men from the area are drawn to the army, and are known for their tough, disciplined efficiency as soldiers. It is also the home of many important businessmen, who may be engaged in commerce and industry almost anywhere in India but still maintain large ancestral estates in the region. I spent three days there; Jai met many ex-soldiers and discussed their problems with them while I was busy campaigning, learning to overcome my timidity and beginning for the first time to feel the warm excitement of communicating with a sympathetic audience.

Jai and I drove to a number of different towns and villages in a car where there was a road and by jeep where there were only country tracks. All the people had been alerted about our arrival and had put up welcoming arches over the roads. They crowded our route, called out to us and often stopped the car or jeep to offer us fresh fruits and vegetables. Sometimes they sang for us and performed the local folk-dances. Always their speeches of welcome were in the most flowery language they could summon.

Gradually I got used to addressing large meetings, backing up the local candidates with a brief description of the new party we were starting and asking the villagers to help us by giving us their votes. Sometimes I quite forgot the crowds and hardly paid attention to the other speakers, gazing instead at the beautifully painted murals which decorate the houses in the towns of that desolate area. The doors were made of some kind of heavy silvery metal, carved and decorated and one could see that although the land was poor agriculturally, still a lot of wealth made by merchants elsewhere in India was brought back to their home district and spent on schools and colleges, as well as the lovely façades of private homes.

During the next two months I covered hundreds of miles mostly by jeep, campaigning more for other candidates than for myself and I discovered with wonderment that the mere hint of my arrival in the remotest sections of the state guaranteed a crowd beyond anything I had imagined. I generally started out at six in the morning and returned to wherever I was staying at midnight or later. I slept under all kinds of conditions and in all sorts of places. I took my own bedding and can never forget the luxury of finding clean sheets and a soft pillow after the long, strenuous day. Bathrooms were something I couldn't arrange, and they turned out to be almost anything—a wooden stool and a bucket of water mostly, sometimes not even that. I remember being intensely grateful when there happened to be a government rest-house in any village where I was to spend the night, or if there was a minor noble or big landowner in the vicinity, living in one of the many small forts that dot the Jaipur landscape. At least then I could be sure that my accommodations would be clean however spartan.

On these tours, my election team and I had to stop nearly every half hour in a village or small town, whether we had planned it or not, and we were often shockingly late for scheduled appearances. Astonishingly, the crowd never seemed to mind the long delays. In the manner of all Indian crowds, they managed to make an impromptu festival out of waiting for my arrival. Sweets stalls arose magically on the outskirts, children rushed about, the women in their festival clothes squatted in groups on the ground, gossiping and exchanging news, and village entertainers diverted the audience during the wait. It was all marvellously good-humoured and patient.

I thought it best to appear on these occasions dressed as simply as possible. So I wore my usual chiffon saris but without ostentatious jewellery—just a pearl necklace and glass bangles on my wrists. But I found that when the villagers gathered around to see their Maharani, they were disappointed; the women, particularly, were horrified that I was wearing virtually no jewellery, not even the anklets that the poorest women among them would certainly own.

Added to the rigours of my touring—the heat, the dust, the long distances travelled in jolting jeeps over desert tracks and winding, unsurfaced village roads—was the problem of the speeches themselves. Although I had never learnt Hindi properly, I could read the Devnagari script. Consequently, I wrote all my speeches first in English, had them translated and written out for me ahead of time, and laboriously learnt them by heart. By the end of the campaign I had managed to understand enough to anticipate the most frequent questions and was even able to answer them in my broken Hindi, struggling and stuttering into the microphone, but managing without a script and with enough confidence to pass for spontaneity.

The whole campaign was perhaps, the most extraordinary period of my life. Seeing and meeting the people of Jaipur, as I did then, I began to realize how little I really knew of the villagers' way of life. The world is too apt to think of India as covered by a blanket of poverty, without any variation except for the very rich. Contrary to this picture, I found that most villagers, despite the simplicity of their lives and the cruel experiences of famine and crop failure, possess a dignity and self-respect that are striking and have a deep security in an inclusive philosophy of life that made me feel both admiration and, in a way, almost envy. Their attitude was far removed from the cringing poverty and whining beggars of the urban slums of Delhi, Bombay, or Calcutta.

Hospitality is one of their great traditions; they would have offered it to any stranger in their village, even if he were merely passing through and had stopped only to ask directions to the next town. Wherever my election team and I went, we were given glasses of milk, tea, or precious water, had sweets and baskets of fresh fruit pressed on us, and were then offered fresh peas or whatever vegetables were in season, to take for sustenance on our further journey. I learnt immediately that water was the most important element in their lives. A good monsoon meant comparative wealth, perhaps a new bicycle or—luxury—a transistor radio. A failure of the rains meant hunger, dying livestock, and possibly death for the family too. Drought is far from rare in Rajasthan, and in the old days the maharajas made arrangements in advance, by seeing to it that water and grain were taken to railheads where villagers could collect them and that camps provided with fodder were set up along the roads to receive migrating cattle. But after the merger states with the Indian Union, these measures no longer seemed urgent to the new government. Emergency measures were neglected when there was no longer a personal involvement of the authorities with the people, and the villagers of Rajasthan suffered more terribly than ever before.

That year, 1962, admittedly, more wells were being dug, but the water was far beneath the surface. Schemes for rural electrification which ideally, could have solved the problem, were slow in developing and even now have not reached more than an eighth of the state. As we drove along the narrow sandy tracks of the villagers past miles and miles of sun-baked earth, every now and again with a sense of delighted surprise we would pass splashes of brilliant green where the construction of a well had actually been successful and had created a thriving wheat or millet field in the middle of comparative desert. Often, as we travelled through the countryside with only an occasional bullock-cart or camel in sight, it seemed unbelievable that all this brown emptiness should be part of one of the most densely populated countries in the world. Then, as we arrived in one of the villages tucked away behind mud walls, the men, women and children would pour out of their houses and I would notice with sadness how the children far outnumbered the adults.

After such tours I would return to Rajmahal exhausted, dusty, wanting nothing so much as a civilized bath and sleep, to find guests—sometimes VIPs—assembled for a dinner-party. I was well past apologizing for my dishevelled appearance and I sometimes had a drink with them and then went up to bed, leaving Jai to cope with the rest of the evening. The only emotion I was capable of registering was relief to be in clean, comfortable surroundings. I was quite unable to conduct the ordinary small-talk that had been a requisite of so much of my social life. If anything, I kept thinking of how much I longed to take all our friends to *show* them this other life that I was discovering. Occasionally I tried to describe it—without too much success and was met for the most part with blank or indulgent attitudes of incredulity. Jai really understood, appreciated, and encouraged me.

Most of the meals were picnics, food taken with us and eaten at any convenient moment. To begin with my election agent had tried to arrange our programme to allow for luncheon stops in the neighbourhood of one of the landlords who, of course, would invite all twenty or of us to share a midday meal with his family. But I soon found that these occasions took up so much time—two hours or so, while the proper courtesies were being extended—that I ruled them out of our programme. I may have offended some people, but it seemed much more important to spend that valuable time with the villagers, hearing their problems, answering their questions and generally getting to approach some realistic acquaintance with the people of Jaipur. Sometimes one or another of the local land lords hearing of our arrival, would set up a lavish banquet with great *thals* of delicious food which we couldn't resist, but after a few times of having to struggle sleepily back into the jeep to get on to our next stop, learned to refuse these invitations as graciously as I could manage. Such banquets included our drivers, elections workers and all the retinue, but if they were disappointed at my cancelling of these delicious breaks in our gruelling routine, they never mentioned it to me.

I think the greatest surprise of the campaign was not the glimpse of 'how the other half lived' but the astonishing fact that I was witnessing and was a part of, what I can only describe as a campaign of love. Everywhere I went I was met with welcome arches, with groups of women singing songs of welcome, with decorations—all the signs of celebration. All these were offered not only to me but to Pat and Joey and to any connection of the Jaipur ruling family. It was intensely moving and at the same time, alarming. It was only when I saw the jubilant, trusting reaction of the crowds—many of whom had walked as much as fifty miles to attend our meetings—that I began to grasp the full extent of the responsibilities we had taken upon ourselves.

The one trap that I was determined to avoid was that of a politician's false promises. I was often urged to make a more effective speech, opening all kinds of attractive futures for the villagers if they would vote for us. But I replied that I couldn't. These were the people of Jaipur and if I owed them nothing else, I certainly owed them the truth. For me in any case, it was much simpler not to lie. I didn't have much of an idea of agriculture, or animal husbandry, or any of their problems in these areas, but at least I could listen and learn and, above all, not offer them impossible future wealth and freedom from hardship. I knew that in the old days apart from a levy on produce, they had paid no taxes and had grazed their camels, bullocks, cows, and goats free on the common pastures, and I knew that now they had to pay a small sum to the Government for each animal—a sum that mounted oppressively by the end of every year. But I only became aware of the dangers of our position when Pat, who was extremely level-headed and practical said, early in the campaign, "Do you know one thing? These people are probably going to vote for us and if we win, do you know what they expect? They expect that suddenly their taxes will vanish, prices will drop, water will miraculously appear in the wells, and everything will be wonderful. And then," he demanded, "what are you going to do?"

I knew that it wasn't much use trying to tell them that they were now living in a democracy, that the most we could do was to air their grievances and try to get some action from the

Government, but that, unhappily, we could guarantee nothing. They couldn't believe these harsh truths. Their response was apt to be the traditional, almost feudal one of saying, in effect, *You* are responsible for us. *You* are our mother and our father. *You* will see that we are properly taken care of.

My decision to stand for Parliament had made a considerable impact both abroad and at home. It had attracted comment in the foreign press—'Maharani fights democratic election' and other such headlines—and often I was followed by television cameras when I was campaigning. Some of them picked up what was to me, the most important facet of the campaign, the warm welcome I received from the villagers because they were sure that I genuinely wanted to help them. They knew that by standing for the Opposition I could benefit neither myself nor my family. As I look back on it, my most cherished memory is the conviction that the people had of our good intentions and the affection they expressed towards all of us.

On the evening before the campaign was to close, the Congress, the Jana Sangh (the extreme rightists), and the Swatantra each held a final meeting in Jaipur. The place chosen by the Swatantra Party was the ground behind the City Palace, where the festival processions took place. The area could hold about two hundred thousand people, about twenty times more than the squares chosen by the Congress and the Jana Sangh. I was worried that with the rival political parties holding their meetings at the same time, the area we had chosen might be too big. To my amazed pleasure, the ground was completely full.

We had invited Jai to speak, along with three lawyers who were standing for election from the city and myself. The Congress Party, in competition, had organized a procession of Indian film stars and had added a maharani—the Maharani of Patiala—to campaign for them. The Jana Sangh was more sober, relying on the attraction of their orthodox Hindu platform to draw an audience. Nevertheless, our meeting broke all records. The three lawyers were all good speakers, and they led off our meeting. I was determined to make the best speech of my life, but in the end I was so afraid and anxious that I think it was the worst one I ever gave.

Then Jai spoke. I was alarmed when he began by addressing the huge crowd by the familiar *tu* for I thought they might resent it. But he was speaking to them as he had always done in all his years as maharaja, accepting the traditional relationship as of a father to his children. "For generations," he said, "my family have ruled you, and we have built up many generations of affection. The new government has taken my state from me, but for all I care they can take the shirt off my back as long as I can keep that bond of trust and affection. They accuse me of putting up my wife and two of my sons for election. They say that if I had a hundred and seventy-six sons"—176 was the number of electoral seats in the Rajasthan Assembly—"that I would put them all up too. But they don't know, do they"—he made a disarming, confidential gesture to the crowd—"that I have far more than only one hundred and seventy-six sons?"

At this there was an enormous, swelling roar from the crowd. Then the people, in high excitement and joy, threw flowers at us, and we threw them back in a mood of spontaneous gaiety. That was the moment at which I knew that I would be elected.

At last the polling day arrived. Baby, Menaka, and other friends who had come to be with me through the end of the campaign had often said, in a hopeless way, "But they don't know what they're *doing*!" as they helped me to explain the election procedure to groups of women. Since most of India is illiterate, at the polls people vote according to a visual symbol of their party. The Congress Party had two bullocks yoked together as a symbol of co-operative endeavor, the Socialists had a spreading banyan tree with its aerial roots to symbolize the spreading growth of socialism, the Communists had the familiar sickle with three stalks of wheat substituted for the hammer, and so on. The Swatantra

Party had a star. Baby, all my other helpers and I spent endless frustrating hours trying to instruct the women about voting for the star. On the ballot sheet, we said, over and over again, this is where the Maharani's name will appear and next to it will be a star. But it was not as simple as that. They noticed a symbol showing a horse and a rider, agreed with each other that the Maharani rides so that must be her symbol. Repeatedly we said, "No, no, that's not the right one." Then they caught sight of the emblem of a flower. Ah, the flower of Jaipur—who else could it mean but the Maharani? "No, no, no, not the flower." All right, the star. Yes, that seems appropriate for the Maharani, but look, here is the sun. If the Maharani is a star, then the sun must certainly mean the Maharaja. We'll vote for both. Immediately the vote would have been invalidated. Even up to the final day, Baby and I were far from sure that we had managed to get our point across.

An Indian election is an uninhibited and joyful event. The women dress up and walk with their husbands and children to the polling booths, singing as they go. Villagers arrive in bullock-carts, the animals garlanded, the carts decorated with flowers and scraps of bright cloth, everybody on holiday and as always, entertainers, sweets-vendors, and storytellers set up their booths near the polling stands to amuse the crowds and make a little money. I drove about through my constituency, spending only a few moments in each place because election laws forbid campaigning twenty-four hours before the actual polling. Since crowds gathered wherever I went, I was afraid I would seem to be breaking the voting laws.

I was made doubly nervous by Jai's telling me that for the honour of the family I had to secure at least five thousand votes more than my nearest rival. And little Jagat sent me a cable from his school in England hoping that I would win by a thousand. That day I sat, unable to put my mind to anything else, simply waiting for news of the election results.

As returns started coming in, my election agent assured me that I was going to win by a tremendous majority and that we should plan a victory procession. Superstitiously, because so presumptuous an idea seemed to be tempting fate, I postponed thinking about it and only after I learned that we had already won nineteen seats did I begin the arrangements for the procession. Pat and Joey had both won (Joey had defeated the incumbent Home Minister), and in all the Jaipur District only a single Congress Party man had been elected.

Finally the results of my election were announced. I had won by a majority of 175,000 votes over the runner-up, the Congress candidate. All my opponents had been forced to forfeit their deposits.

ACKNOWLEDGMENTS

Excerpt from *The Queen of Jhansi* by Mahasweta Devi, translated by Sagaree and Mandira Sengupta, is reprinted with the permission of Seagull Books.

'The Room of Many Colours' by Ruskin Bond is reprinted with the permission of the author.

'Rani Jindan Kaur' and 'The Maharanis of Travancore' are reproduced by arrangement with HarperCollins Publishers India Private Limited from the books *The Last Queen* by Chitra Banerjee Divakaruni and *The Ivory Throne* by Manu S. Pillai in English and first published by them. All rights reserved. Unauthorized copying is strictly prohibited.

The First Spring: Life in the Golden Age of India by Abraham Eraly was first published in 2014. Excerpt reprinted with the permission of Penguin Random House India.

'The Controversial Queen of Kashmir' was originally published in *The Women Who Ruled India* by Archana Garodia Gupta in 2019 and is excerpted with permission from Hachette India.

Excerpt from *Heroines: Powerful Indian Women of Myth and History* by Ira Mukhoty is reprinted with the permission of the author.

A Begum and A Rani: Hazrat Mahal and Lakshmibai in 1857 by Rudrangshu Mukherjee was first published in 2021. Excerpt reprinted with the permission of Penguin Random House India.

Empress: The Astonishing Reign of Nur Jahan by Ruby Lal was first published in 2018. Excerpt reprinted with the permission of Penguin Random House India.

The Princess and the Political Agent by Binodini was first published in 2020. Excerpt reprinted with the permission of Penguin Random House India.

Excerpt from *A Princess Remembers: The Memoirs of the Maharani of Jaipur* by Gayatri Devi is reprinted with the permission of Rupa Publications India.

NOTES ON THE CONTRIBUTORS

Abraham Eraly (1934–2015) wrote four acclaimed volumes on pre-modern Indian history—*The Last Spring: The Lives and Times of the Great Mughals*, *Gem in the Lotus: The Seeding of Indian Civilization*, *The First Spring: The Golden Age of India*, and *The Age of Wrath: A History of the Delhi Sultanate*. He taught Indian history in colleges in India and the United States, and was the editor of *Aside*, India's first city magazine.

Archana Garodia Gupta is an author, entrepreneur, and quizzer. She wrote *The Women Who Ruled India* and the co-authored *The History of India for Children* with Shruti Garodia. She runs a successful jewellery business and served as the president of the FICCI Ladies Organization in 2015–2016. She lives in New Delhi.

Chitra Banerjee Divakaruni is the author of several bestselling books including *The Mistress of Spices*, *Sister of My Heart*, *Palace of Illusions*, *The Forest of Enchantments*, and *The Last* Queen. Her work has also appeared in the *Atlantic Monthly*, the *New Yorker*, *Vogue*, *Verve*, *Elle*, Oprah's *O magazine*, *Best American Short Stories*, the *Pushcart Prize Anthology*, and *O Henry Prize Stories*. She has won two Pushcart Prizes, the American Book Award, the PEN Josephine Miles Award, the Allen Ginsberg Poetry Award, the Houston Literary Award, and the Times of India Best Fiction Award among others. She is the McDavid Professor of Creative Writing at the University of Houston. She lives in Houston with her husband and two sons.

Gayatri Devi (1919–2009) was the third Maharani consort of Jaipur through her marriage to Maharaja Sawai Man Singh II. She was the daughter of Maharaja Jitendra Narayan and Maharani Indira Devi of Cooch Behar, West Bengal. After India's independence and the abolition of princely states, she ran for parliament and won the 1962 Lok Sabha election with one of largest landslides in the world. She served the Swatantra Party for twelve years. She died in Jaipur in 2009.

Ira Mukhoty is the author of *Daughters of the Sun: Empresses, Queens and Begums of the Mughal Empire*, *Heroines: Powerful Indian Women in Myth and History*, *Akbar: The Great Mughal*, and *Song of Draupadi: A Novel*. Living in one of the oldest continuously inhabited cities in the world, she developed an interest in the evolution of mythology and history, the erasure of women from these histories, and the continuing relevance this has on the status of women in India. She writes rigorously researched narrative histories that are accessible to the lay reader. She lives in Gurgaon with her husband and two daughters.

L. Somi Roy has translated his mother Binodini's works from Manipuri including the novel *The Princess and the Political Agent*, the play *Crimson Rainclouds*, the screenplay *My Son, My Precious*, and *The Maharaja's Household: A Daughter's Memories of Her Father*. He also founded Imasi: The Maharaj Kumari Binodini Devi Foundation in Imphal. As a film curator based in New York, he has organized exhibitions for the Museum of Modern Art, the film society of Lincoln Center, Whitney Museum of American Art, and Asia Society. He writes on film and culture and works towards the conservation of the Manipuri pony in India.

Maharaj Kumari Binodini Devi (1922–2011) was an award-winning novelist, playwright, and short-story writer. She was the daughter of Maharaja Sir Churachand Singh and Maharani Dhanamanjuri of Manipur and was also known as Princess Wangolsana. Her first collection of short stories, *Nunggairakta Chandramukhi*, won the Jamini Sundar Guha Gold Medal in 1966. She received the Sahitya Akademi Award in 1979 for her novel *Boro Saheb Ongbi Sanatombi*. She also wrote screenplays and song lyrics and several of her works were adapted to films. She died at the age of eighty-eight in Imphal. She was posthumously awarded the Best Story Award at the 9th Manipur State Film Awards for the movie *Nangna Kappa Pakchade* in 2014.

Mahasweta Devi (1926–2016) was an eminent Bengali writer and activist known for her fiction and political writing. Her notable works include *Jhansir Rani*, *Hajar Churashir Maa*, *Rudali*, and *Aranyer Adhikar* (for which she received the Sahitya Akademi Award in 1979). She worked rigorously for the upliftment of tribal people of West Bengal, Bihar, Madhya Pradesh, and Chhattisgarh and was awarded a Padma Shri for her activism in 1986. She was also honoured with the Jnanpith Award,

Ramon Magsaysay Award, and Padma Vibhushan. She died at the age of ninety in Kolkata.

Mandira Sengupta is a translator and artist with an interest in Bengali literature. She has co-translated Mahasweta Devi's *The Book of the Hunter* and *The Queen of Jhansi* with her daughter Sagaree Sengupta.

Manu S. Pillai is the author of the award-winning *The Ivory Throne: Chronicles of the House of Travancore, Rebel Sultans: The Deccan from Khilji to Shivaji*, and *The Courtesan, the Mahatma and the Italian Brahmin: Tales from Indian History*. Formerly Chief of Staff to Dr Shashi Tharoor, MP, he has also worked at the House of Lords in Britain, with Lord Karan Bilimoria CBE, DL, and with the BBC on their *Incarnations* history series. Manu's first book, *The Ivory Throne*, won the 2016 Tata Literature Live First Book Award for non-fiction and the 2017 Sahitya Akademi Yuva Puraskar. Manu has contributed the text to Serena Chopra's *Bhutan Echoes*. His other writings have appeared in *The Hindu*, *Mint Lounge*, *Open Magazine*, the *Times of India*, *Hindustan Times*, and other publications.

Ruby Lal is an acclaimed historian and the author of *Domesticity and Power in the Early Mughal World*, *Coming of Age in Nineteenth Century India: The Girl-Child and the Art of Playfulness*, and *Empress: The Astonishing Reign of Nur Jahan*. She won the 2018 Georgia Author of the Year Award in Biography and was also a finalist in History for the Los Angeles Times Book Prize. She is Professor of South Asian History at Emory University, Atlanta and divides her time between Atlanta and Delhi.

Rudrangshu Mukherjee is Chancellor and Professor of History at Ashoka University of which he was the founding Vice Chancellor. He was educated at Calcutta Boys' School, Presidency College, Calcutta, JNU and St Edmund Hall, Oxford. He was awarded a DPhil in Modern History by the University of Oxford. He taught in the department of history, Calcutta University, and held visiting appointments at Princeton University, Manchester University and the University of California, Santa Cruz. From 1993 to 2014 he was the Editor, Editorial Pages, The Telegraph. He is the author of many books—these include *Nehru & Bose: Parallel Lives*; *Awadh in Revolt 1857–58: A Study of Popular Resistance*; *Spectre of Violence: The Massacres in Kanpur in 1857*; *The Year of Blood:*

Essays on 1857, Dateline 1857: Revolt against the Raj. His recent books include *Tagore and Gandhi: Walking Alone, Walking Together* which won the Valley of Words Award 2022, non-fiction, and *Twilight Falls on Liberalism*. He is the editor of *Great Speeches of Modern India* and *The Penguin Gandhi Reader* and the co-author of *New Delhi: The Making of a Capital and India: Then and Now*.

Ruskin Bond is the author of several bestselling novels and collections of short stories, essays, and poems. These include *The Room on the Roof* (winner of the John Llewellyn Rhys Prize); *A Flight of Pigeons*; *The Night Train at Deoli*; *Time Stops at Shamli*; *Our Trees Still Grow in Dehra* (winner of the Sahitya Akademi Award); *Angry River*; *The Blue Umbrella*; *Delhi Is Not Far*; *Rain in the Mountains*; *Tigers for Dinner*; *Tales of Fosterganj*; *A Gathering of Friends*; *Upon an Old Wall Dreaming*; *Small Towns, Big Stories*; *Unhurried Tales*; *A Gallery of Rascals*; *Rhododendrons in the Mist*; *Miracle at Happy Bazaar* (winner of Kalinga Literary Festival Children's Book of the Year 2021); *It's a Wonderful Life*; *The Shadow on the Wall*; and *Song of the Forest*. He was awarded the Padma Shri by the Government of India in 1999, a Lifetime Achievement Award by the Delhi government in 2012, and the Padma Bhushan in 2014. He was selected for the prestigious Sahitya Akademi Fellowship in 2021.

Sagaree Sengupta has co-translated Mahasweta Devi's *The Book of the Hunter* and *The Queen of Jhansi*. She teaches South Asian languages and literature at the University of Wisconsin-Madison.